Even something small
can be a big clue.

I smiled. "We're slowly but surely compiling evidence." I took the flashlight back from Henry. "Maybe there's something else out here that might help." We continued to walk in circles—concentric circles—each one bigger than the last. We were determined to find anything that might lead us to Mr., or rather, Mrs. Big.

"What's that over there?" Henry said.

I aimed the flashlight in the direction he was pointing. There was a piece of paper, crumpled up, on the ground. I retrieved it, opened it, and held it out for both of us to see.

"Another note . . . in code," Henry said.

Like the last one, this note also appeared to be written in lipstick. And like before, there was a series of nonsensical letters and numbers on it.

OTHER BOOKS YOU MAY ENJOY

CHARLIE COLLIER

= SNOOP FOR HIRE =

The Homemade Stuffing Caper

JOHN MADORMO

PUFFIN BOOKS
An Imprint of Penguin Group (USA) Inc.

PUFFIN BOOKS
Published by the Penguin Group
Penguin Young Readers Group, 345 Hudson Street, New York, New York 10014, U.S.A.
Penguin Group (Canada), 90 Eglinton Avenue East, Suite 700, Toronto, Ontario, Canada M4P 2Y3
(a division of Pearson Penguin Canada Inc.)
Penguin Books Ltd, 80 Strand, London WC2R 0RL, England
Penguin Ireland, 25 St Stephen's Green, Dublin 2, Ireland (a division of Penguin Books Ltd)
Penguin Group (Australia), 250 Camberwell Road, Camberwell, Victoria 3124, Australia
(a division of Pearson Australia Group Pty Ltd)
Penguin Books India Pvt Ltd, 11 Community Centre, Panchsheel Park, New Delhi – 110 017, India
Penguin Group (NZ), 67 Apollo Drive, Rosedale, Auckland 0632, New Zealand
(a division of Pearson New Zealand Ltd.)
Penguin Books (South Africa) (Pty) Ltd, 24 Sturdee Avenue,
Rosebank, Johannesburg 2196, South Africa

Penguin Books Ltd, Registered Offices: 80 Strand, London WC2R 0RL, England

First published in the United States of America by Philomel,
a division of Penguin Young Readers Group, 2012
Published by Puffin Books, a member of Penguin Young Readers Group, 2013

1 3 5 7 9 10 8 6 4 2

Copyright © John V. Madormo, 2012
All rights reserved

THE LIBRARY OF CONGRESS HAS CATALOGED THE PHILOMEL BOOKS EDITION AS FOLLOWS:
Madormo, John V. Charlie Collier, snoop for hire :
the homemade stuffing caper / John V. Madormo.
p. cm.
Summary: Twelve-year-old Charlie's analytical skills win him few friends at school,
but when the most popular girl in class comes to the makeshift private investigation
office in his parents' garage asking Charlie's help to find her missing bird,
he and friend Henry begin their first real case.
ISBN 978-0-399-25543-4
[1. Private investigators—Fiction. 2. Lost and found possessions—Fiction. 3. Birds—Fiction.
4. Family life—Illinois—Fiction. 5. Grandmothers—Fiction. 6. Illinois—Fiction.
7. Mystery and detective stories.] I. Title. II. Title: Homemade stuffing caper.
PZ7.M26574Ch 2012 [Fic]—dc23 2011013064

Puffin Books ISBN 978-0-14-242380-6

Design by Amy Wu
Text set in ITC New Baskerville

Printed in the United States of America

All rights reserved. No part of this book may be reproduced, scanned, or distributed in any
printed or electronic form without permission. Please do not participate in or encourage piracy
of copyrighted materials in violation of the author's rights. Purchase only authorized editions.

To my wife, Celeste,
for her endless love,
support, and encouragement.

CHAPTER 1

The Bouncing Czechs Caper

The name's Collier. Charlie Collier. Glad to meet you. Maybe you've heard of me. No? That's hard to believe. Well, then you're one of the few folks in Oak Grove, Illinois, who hasn't. I'm practically a legend— at least at Roosevelt Middle School, that is. Everybody knows me there. You see, I help folks—for a price that is. Take Josh Hartley, sixth-grade class president, for instance. When Josh was falsely accused of a crime he didn't commit, he sought out my services. And who do you suppose identified the *real* culprit who dumped live goldfish into the principal's water cooler? Yep, that was me. When Tracy Hudson, cheerleader captain, found herself on the hot seat, she called me too. And who do you think exposed the *real* perpetrator who teepeed the teachers' lounge? Yep, me again.

Does any of this stuff ring a bell? No? Why don't you check me out—on the Internet. I'm the big kid—yeah, the big kid with the XXL wardrobe. I carry a little extra muscle. Well, it's not really muscle, but I like to call it that. Oh, I'm not saying I enjoy being fat. There I go again, using that word. My mom makes me put a quarter in the vacation jar every time I say it. But it doesn't really bother me. It's who I am. Don't get me wrong, if I could snap my fingers and shed thirty pounds, I'd certainly do it. It's just that I've tried so many times. Diets, exercise programs, even hypnosis. Nothing's worked. This is my lot in life and I've accepted it. After all, it's in the genes. Take a good look at my parents. I never had a chance. But I don't blame them. I don't blame anyone.

As a matter of fact, a few extra pounds can come in mighty handy in my line of work. Sometimes you need to get tough. Push people around. But there's a reason for it. I'm a private eye. You know—a detective, investigator, shamus. Whatever you want to call it. I don't act in an official capacity—I mean, after all, I'm only twelve years old—but I've got a nice little business going.

I think I was about ten when I realized that I had this gift. These powers of deduction. On the playground, I was always the first one to unravel a riddle. In the classroom, a word problem was no problem. I didn't even have to think. It was a little scary—almost as if my brain had a mind of its own. Stuff just seemed to pop into my head.

For a long time I wondered how these skills would

pay off. Then a friend of mine, actually my best friend, Henry Cunningham, gave me an idea.

"You know, Charlie, I'll bet folks would pay for a service like this."

"What do you mean?"

"Solving mysteries for people."

"Like what?"

"Like what? Finding out who stuffed you into a locker, who stole your lunch money, or who put fake barf on your desk. Heck, I'd pay to find out."

The more I thought about it, the more I realized Henry was right. It was a great idea. This was an untapped market. There were people in need. Damsels in distress. Paying customers. How could I refuse? Someone had to come to their aid. Why not me?

In the past few months, I've managed to grow a fairly successful business. All out of our garage. It's the perfect office. I'm open for business only when my parents are out of the house. And I've a built a pretty impressive client list. You'd be surprised how many kids want dirt on their classmates.

I have my scruples, of course. After all, I'm Charlie Collier, Snoop for Hire, not some Peeping Tom. I'll have you know I've turned down my share of cases. Like the time Kevin O'Keefe wanted to know why Mr. Summers, our gym coach, seemed to have no butt. As far as I was concerned, that was no one's business. Although to ease my own curiosity, I did happen to discover that he had been the victim of a liposuction procedure gone horribly wrong. It all seemed to fit. There had to have been a malpractice suit that had produced a tidy sum. How else would you explain the Porsche he drove around the school parking lot? But there were just some things that the public need not know.

And so my life as a junior sleuth is proceeding rather nicely. Not to mention that when clients seek out my services, they look at me as a solution to their problems, not just some weight-challenged kid. Weight-challenged . . . yeah, my mom's okay with that one.

When one of my clients smiled and shook my hand one day following a rather challenging case, I soon discovered the secret of surviving the battle of the waistline. I realized that when people look at you for who you are, and not for your appearance, it makes a whole lotta difference. It was at that moment that I saw the light. I decided that, since I would probably never be lean and mean, instead I would always place myself in a position to offer a necessary service to my fellow man. I wanted people to see me for what I could accomplish. It's worked. And, you know, I decided that even if I ever do shed these pounds, it'll still be a pretty good way to live my life.

Well, back to what really matters: solving cases for your fellow man—and making a few bucks. It's not easy, you know. Running a detective agency is a lot of work. It helps to have a partner—and I have the best. Henry's job is to book clients and handle the finances. And he's pretty easygoing—unless someone tries to stiff us, of course. To Henry, a satisfied customer is one who pays on time. If not, watch out. Collections is one of his strong suits. Simply put, Henry is the agency muscle—short for his age, but as tough as anyone twice his size.

Henry and I were together, in the garage as always, about a week or so ago. It had been a quiet day and we were about to close up shop. The garage had seemed particularly dusty. Henry carefully rolled a dart between his thumb and forefinger. He had recently learned the rules of English darts, and it made him feel worldly. He eyed his target, bit his bottom lip, cleared his throat, and let loose.

"Did you see that? A triple-seventeen," he said.

"Shhhh." I wasn't downplaying his achievement, I was just wrapped up in what I can only describe as my passion, or what Henry would call my obsession . . . Sam Solomon, Private Eye, a series of detective novels set in Chicago in the 1930s. I carefully cradled Episode #11—*The Bouncing Czechs Caper*—and ever so delicately turned pages as if they were pieces of priceless parchment. I wanted to savor each cunning feat of deduction, each moment of unthinkable peril.

Sam Solomon was my hero. He was responsible for

who I was, who I dreamed of becoming. He was the master of mystery. When working on a case of my own, I would always think to myself: What would Sam do? And within seconds, I had the answer.

So, why would Henry even think of disturbing a student in the midst of intense research?! It was unthinkable, untimely, and just plain rude.

"How many times have you read that one? You already know what happens," he said.

It was not a question I chose to answer. Instead I shot back with one of my own. "What's the combination of Sam Solomon's safe?"

Henry threw his head back and fired the remaining handful of darts at the board. "I don't know."

"Twenty-six—nine—thirty-seven."

"Now why would I care about that?"

"You never know when something like that'll come in handy."

Henry, as was his style, waved me off, then seemed to think for a moment, and smiled. "Okay, genius, try this. I found it on the Web. How many animals of each species did Moses take on the ark?" Henry seemed particularly proud of himself.

I could only shake my head. This was clearly an amateur's attempt to trip up the master. Now, I don't mean to sound cocky, but if you had spent the better part of your twelve years solving puzzles, you would know that the first step in solving a riddle is to dismiss the obvious. And in this riddle, the first move was to reject the element of mathematics. This wasn't a numbers question. One had to analyze each word of the statement. The answer was obvious.

"Moses wasn't on the ark," I said. "Noah was."

Henry closed his eyes tightly and groaned. It was a familiar sound. He had yet to stump me, but it didn't stop him from trying. I admired that. Every so often, I considered missing one, but I always suspected that he would know, and that would be embarrassing. Henry wanted to best me one day, more than anything, but he'd never take charity. Whenever I managed to decipher one of his riddles, which he scoured the Internet for on a daily basis, he would fire back with some comment about my lack of interest in technology.

Henry stewed for a moment. He needed a comeback in the worst way. He had to save face. "Well . . . well . . . you call this a modern-day detective agency?" he said. "Where are our cell phones—our GPS navigation systems—our digital audio recorders? Huh? Just think how much more effective we'd be with those at our disposal."

"I've told you before—Sam Solomon didn't need them—and we don't need them. We solve our cases with good old-fashioned *think* technology. We don't need any of those gadgets," I said.

A knock at the door interrupted the standoff. I

looked at Henry. We weren't expecting anyone, especially at the end of the day. Henry grabbed a clipboard off the workbench and shrugged his shoulders.

"You sure you didn't book anyone?" I asked.

Henry shook his head. "Nope."

We needed our game faces on . . . and fast. I grabbed my trench coat, hanging on a hook that it shared with a bamboo rake. It was a wrinkled beige number that my dad thought he had donated to Goodwill.

Henry darted to the far corner of the garage and tried to pry loose an old, tattered card table, stuck behind an aluminum ladder. "Help me with this."

"Be right there," I assured our uninvited guest. I scooted over to aid Henry. One good yank and the table was free, but we had inadvertently knocked the ladder from its supports, directly onto my toe. "Oh man!"

Another knock at the door. Henry placed his hand over my mouth to muffle the groans. "Just a minute . . . ," he yelled.

We quickly set up the wobbly, makeshift desk. Hopping on one foot, I slid a pair of lawn chairs up next to it, and placed a legal pad and pencil on the table.

"Ready?" Henry asked as he grasped the doorknob.

"Wait a minute. Something's not right." I quickly scanned the area. Everything seemed to be in place. Why did I feel incomplete, undressed?

Henry snapped his fingers. "Your hat." He pointed

to a black fedora hanging on a hook next to some garden tools.

I ran over, carefully fitted it onto my oversize noggin, glanced into a broken mirror, pulled the brim down slightly, and nodded confidently at Henry.

As the door creaked open, I turned around, and my eyes beheld a vision. Standing in the entranceway was our classmate Scarlett Alexander, a statuesque beauty in a sequined jean jacket. Scarlett flashed a killer smile and walked in, flicking her hair as she passed by. She held a cell phone to her ear—a familiar sight. She was never without it.

"I'm going to have to call you back, Sarah. I have an appointment," she said as she flipped off her phone.

Henry glanced at me and rolled his eyes. Henry was not what you would call Scarlett's biggest fan. He always thought that she used her looks, not her brains, to get her through tough scrapes. That mattered little to me. I had been smitten since kindergarten. And I think I can speak for the entire male population of the sixth grade class—minus Henry, of course—when I say that each of us hoped, even prayed, for Scarlett just to look in our direction, let alone speak our names. Henry, amazingly, was unfazed. It might as well have been the janitor walking in.

At times, I envied him. I always wished I could have been more like Henry—in complete control—instead of a babbling idiot whenever a pretty girl walked in the room. At that moment, as Scarlett was passing by, her perfume trail nearly choked both of us, but there was something about it that made you yearn for more. I knew I should have followed Henry's lead, but like Sam Solomon, I was hooked the minute a mysterious woman entered the office.

"H-H-Hello. Can I help you?" I could barely spit it out.

"I hope so," Scarlett said softly. "Can I sit down?"

I slid out the lawn chair. Its metal bottom scraped the cement floor. Scarlett lowered herself delicately into the seat and crossed her legs. I plopped down in a chair opposite hers. It was at that moment, as the chair was collapsing beneath me and I was falling to the ground, that I remembered the missing screw in the lawn chair I had so unfortunately chosen.

Scarlett snickered as I climbed to my feet and brushed myself off. I thought it best to say nothing, to maintain my professionalism, but this was certainly no way to impress a new client, let alone the most popular girl in class. Scarlett was no ordinary sixth-grader. She had seventh grade–second semester written all over her.

She turned away for a moment, allowing me to save face. She looked in Henry's direction, and he returned a scowl. Then she smiled politely at me. I could hardly believe it. There she was—in my garage. I was going to enjoy the moment. I cleared my throat as Henry slid another chair over to the table. I pushed down on the seat before settling in.

"So what can I do for you?" I asked.

"I need your help," she said.

"Of course. What seems to be the problem?"

"It has to do with a missing person. Well, it's not really a person."

I began scribbling on the notepad. "Why don't you tell me about it."

"By the way, how much do you charge?" she said.

But before I could answer, Henry stepped in. He was holding the change jar.

"Excuse me, Charlie, this is my territory," he announced.

Scarlett rolled her eyes.

"A missing person's case is certainly more diffi-cult than others," he said. "It requires a great deal of resources—"

"It's not a missing *person*," she snapped.

"Nevertheless," Henry continued, without taking a breath, "my partner and I will be forced to log untold man hours . . ."

"How much?" she said, gritting her teeth.

I needed to defuse the situation. "We really don't know until we hear all the details," I said. "It's hard to say." I turned to Henry. "Let's get more info before we set a price, okay?"

Henry threw up his arms. "Whatever."

I smiled politely at Scarlett. "Please continue."

She glared at Henry and uncrossed her legs.

The next sound I had expected to hear was Scarlett's soft, lulling voice. But instead a grinding noise froze me. My head dropped. The moment had been shattered.

"Aw, Mom," I whined, as the garage door began to rise. The family minivan pulled in and stopped abruptly. I motioned for Henry and Scarlett to follow me out the side door.

"Listen, Scarlett, I gotta go," I said.

"But I didn't have a chance to tell you about my problem," she said. "It's important."

"It'll have to wait. I'll talk to you at school or something."

Scarlett huffed, spun around, and was off.

I knew this was no way to treat a customer, but what choice did I have? I looked around for Henry. He was long gone. He knew the drill.

A short time later, minus trench coat and fedora, I marched through the back door without acknowledging my mother. I hadn't gotten more than a few steps into the kitchen when I felt her tugging at the back of my shirt.

"Hey, just what were you doing in the garage?"

This was more than a simple question. It had all the signs of a full-blown interrogation.

"Nothing."

"And who was that girl with you and Henry? I didn't recognize her."

"Nobody." The woman was now on dangerous grounds. There were certain topics that were simply not discussed. Months before, I had placed both of my parents on a strict need-to-know basis. Information regarding girls was classified. Period.

"Please don't tell me you're at it again," my mother said.

I locked my jaw and stared at my shoes.

"Honey, believe me, I understand. You think you're offering some valuable service to your friends." Her voice softened. "But at whose expense?"

I had told myself that if my mother brought up this topic again, I would simply ignore it. But someone had to inform this woman that I had a gift. It would be wrong . . . selfish not to share it.

"Mom, kids seek me out. I'm just trying to feed their need."

"Do you remember what happened when you hid a camera in the boys' bathroom at school?"

"One of my most successful cases," I answered proudly.

"You got suspended."

She just didn't get it. What was it going to take to win her over?

"You forget," I said. "We found out who was stealing all of the urinal cakes."

"Who cares about urinal cakes?"

"I see you haven't spent much time in a boys' bathroom." I waved my hand in front of my nose and made a face, just for effect.

"Oh, I give up," she said.

I took that as permission to exit. My mother, however, was far from finished. She quickly caught up and spun me around.

"Listen, mister, I don't want to get any calls from school or the neighbors or—"

"Don't worry, Mom," I interrupted. "I'll be discreet."

"'Discreet'? Do you even know what that word means?"

"Of course," I assured her. "*Discreet*. Adjective. Demonstrating prudence and wise self-restraint in speech and behavior." I smiled.

She shook her head and stormed off.

Victory!

CHAPTER 2

The Idol Hands Caper

With only a week remaining before spring break, I sat in Mrs. Jansen's science class daydreaming about a mystery client who would walk into the office with a case that would tax my brain like no other. But it was only a dream. At least I was sitting in the right place if I wanted a little brain stimulation. Mrs. Jansen always made us think. For a science teacher she was all right—mid-thirties, relatively attractive. Most science teachers, if you haven't noticed, are either skinny, bald men, or old ladies with nicknames like Scab. Mrs. Jansen was different. But in order to survive one of her classes, you had better be a learner, not a lounger. She had the ability to calm the restless, and was truly a wizard at awakening a sleeping giant—a class just back from lunch—especially when the lights were low.

"Now, who can tell me what this bird is?" she asked as she changed to the next image in her slide presentation.

We were face-to-face with one scary-looking dude. It had brown and white spots all over and a sharp beak that bent downward. I wouldn't want to tangle with this fellow on a dark night, that was for sure. Mrs. Jansen stared into a sea of drooping eyelids. There was no response from the assembled group of nearly comatose kids.

Sensing she was losing her audience, Mrs. Jansen did not wait for a response. "It's called an American peregrine falcon. And like the northern spotted owl and the imperial parrot, they are all on the endangered species list. We must do everything in our power to help preserve these beautiful creatures." She paused momentarily and sighed. "I'm not sure if any of you saw the newspaper story the other day but one of these magnificent falcons has mysteriously disappeared from a wildlife sanctuary in the area. I can't imagine who would do something like that." She shook her head and flipped on the lights.

She was met by the groans and gripes of students who were now forced to leave their vegetative state and pay attention.

"Okay, we'd better change the subject," Mrs. Jansen said. "We don't have much time left in the period."

I was hoping this wouldn't take long. I had arranged to meet up with a very important client after school— Scarlett.

"Now, who can tell me what pollination is?" Twenty-five sets of eyes dropped to their desks. "Does this sound familiar? The transfer of pollen from the flower's stamen to its pistil." More blank stares. "Let's see if a little game of mystery can generate some interest in this topic."

With the mention of *mystery,* all eyes turned to me. I was slightly uncomfortable with the attention. Then Sherman Doyle, a six-foot, 250-pounder, raised his hand. Sherman was not what you would call an academic giant. His strength was his physical presence.

"Yes, Sherman," Mrs. Jansen said.

"Don't call on Charlie for the answer, okay?"

Comments from others in the class seemed to agree. "Yeah, let *us* do it this time."

Mrs. Jansen appeared grateful for their enthusiasm, but not with the conditions. "Well, that doesn't seem quite fair, now does it?"

"He's got one of them anatomical brains," Sherman said. "It's too easy for him."

"Do you mean *analytical*, Sherman?"

"That's what I said."

It made little sense to join this conversation. I buried my nose in a book. If they didn't want me to participate, that was okay. I was happy enough just to observe.

Mrs. Jansen was now staring at me. "It seems your reputation has preceded you, Mr. Collier."

I shrugged my shoulders and kept silent.

"Okay, class, here's the premise." Mrs. Jansen began

waving her hands in front of the blackboard. "Imagine this entire wall covered with flowers . . . identical flowers. But only one is real. The rest are artificial."

I felt my heart race. Even if I couldn't answer it, I loved the challenge.

"Without coming up and touching or smelling any of them, how can you tell which one is the real flower?"

There was no response from anyone in class. I fought the urge to raise my hand. The answer was so obvious. Surely someone would unravel this brain buster. Mrs. Jansen scanned the room slowly. There was a pained expression on her face. She seemed disappointed that no one had accepted the challenge. A moment later, she shook her head and sighed.

"Is it all right if I call on Charlie?" she said.

A handful of students turned and stared at me.

"Okay, Charlie, what do you think?" she asked.

At last. This was my chance to shine. But just then, I had second thoughts. Should I show up the other kids again, or just play dumb? A little voice told me to be just one of the guys—to pretend I was as baffled as everyone else in the room. It would pay dividends on the playground. But how could I walk away? Would Sam Solomon have withheld valuable information? In Episode #14— *The Idol Hands Caper*—he shared details of his investigation with local authorities that led to the arrest of a famed archeologist who had stolen priceless relics from the Aztec treasures in Mexico. Sam couldn't stand pat, and neither can I.

"Well?" She was waiting for my response. "Don't tell me we've stumped you too?!"

I looked into the anxious and jealous eyes of my classmates. What was I afraid of? I took a deep breath and stood up.

"This is how I see it," I said. "I'd open the window and wait for a bee to fly into the room. Then, whichever flower it lands on, that's the real one." I sat back down quickly.

A roomful of heads turned and awaited Mrs. Jansen's response. She just smiled and nodded. "That's it."

A mixture of cheers and jeers filled the room. I appreciated the kudos from Mrs. Jansen and from *some* of my classmates. But the reaction from the others made me second-guess my decision to speak up. I might just have to fight that urge in the future. As great as it was to nail a brain buster, it didn't quite make up for the feelings of rejection from some.

Henry and I met up after school on the edge of the playground as always. He was busy playing a handheld video game. I, on the other hand, began to scan the immediate area.

"Are you looking for somebody?" he said.

"Scarlett."

He stared at me. "Scarlett?" he said. "For what?"

I suddenly had his attention. It was the first time his eyes had left the tiny screen in his hands.

"I'm supposed to meet her out here."

Henry appeared confused.

"Remember, in the garage yesterday," I said, "she started to tell us about some missing person or thing?"

"Oh yeah. Whatever," he said with a disinterested look. "Hey, let me ask you something. How'd you figure out that flower thing back in Mrs. Jansen's class?" he asked.

I shrugged. "I don't know. Stuff starts to percolate up here," I said, pointing to my head, "and the answer just pops into my brain. I don't even try sometimes."

"Okay, genius, try this: A clerk in a butcher shop is five-feet, ten-inches tall. What does he weigh?"

I grinned, ready for the challenge. Now, let's see: a five-foot-ten-inch-tall butcher. There clearly was not enough information here to determine an answer as to his weight. Therefore, the answer had to be hidden in the riddle. Best to break it down word by word. What—does—he—*weigh*? I reflected for a moment, then grinned.

"What does he weigh?" I asked.

"Yeah." Henry looked confident, and I knew he was hoping—praying that this was his moment of victory.

"He works in a butcher shop," I said. "So, he weighs . . . *meat*."

Henry threw his head back disgustedly. "Mark my words, Charlie. One of these days, I'm gonna trip you up."

"Thanks for the warning," I said with a smile.

Henry dug into his pocket and pulled out a handful of index cards. "Hey, what do you think of these?"

On each card were printed the words:

CHARLIE COLLIER,
SNOOP FOR HIRE

SPECIAL WEEKEND HOURS THIS SATURDAY
NIGHT UNSOLVABLE PROBLEMS SOLVED
IN SECONDS REASONABLE RATES

BOOK YOUR APPPINTMENT TODAY!

"What do you think? I've been handing 'em out all over school."

But before I could respond, Sherman Doyle appeared.

"Give it a rest in there, Collier," Sherman warned. "You're makin' us look bad."

I wanted to respond with something witty. And I wanted to use words like *big, dumb,* and *ugly.* But all that came out was . . .

"I'm sorry."

"You should be."

I looked away, hoping he would leave. Henry, on the other hand, seemed to welcome confrontation.

"Take a hike," he barked at Sherman.

The oversize sixth-grader grabbed Henry by his belt and lifted him off the ground. "What'd you say, shrimp?" Sherman was now dangling him over a sewer cover.

"I'm not afraid of you," Henry fired back, swinging his arms futilely at his enemy.

Sherman grinned, but when one punch unexpectedly hit its mark, the class bully quickly tired of the game and tossed Henry in my direction. We both toppled to the ground. Sherman laughed as he walked away, then stopped in his tracks. He bent down and scooped up something from the ground.

"Oh no, I hope he's okay," Sherman said quietly.

Henry and I looked at each other, then walked over to Sherman, curious about what had gotten him to show any emotion other than meanness.

Resting in the palm of his hand was a dead bird. He started pressing its chest up and down with his thumb.

"What are you doing?" I said.

"I'm trying to get his little heart going. What do you think I'm doin'?"

"Don't waste your time," Henry said. "He's a goner."

After a few seconds had passed and the bird remained motionless, Sherman sighed, set the creature down gently onto a pile of leaves, and walked away.

Henry and I stood there, in shock at Sherman's display of kindness. "I don't get it," I said. "Why is he so nice to a bird but he hates me?"

"Aw, don't worry about him," Henry said.

"I don't want people to hate me."

"*People* don't hate you, *Sherman* does. There's a difference." Henry chuckled.

"Charlie," a voice called out. It was Scarlett. She came running over. "Can we talk now?"

"Absolutely," I said. I set my backpack on the ground and reached in for a legal pad and something to write with.

I noticed Henry rolling his eyes. He wasn't shy about showing his true feelings for Scarlett.

"Okay, all ready," I said.

But before Scarlett could fill me in, a car with its horn blaring came flying around the corner and screeched to a stop just yards from where we were standing.

I turned to look but Henry grabbed me by the shoulders and spun me back around.

"Better not," he said.

"Why?" I asked. "What's up?"

"Just how were you planning on getting home today?" he said.

"My mom's picking me up."

"You sure about that? Because your grandma just got out of that car."

"Oh no!" I dropped my head and closed my eyes tightly. "What's she wearing this time?"

"Let me put it this way. You don't want to look on an empty stomach."

My grandmother, Constance Collier, was a free spirit to say the least. To know her was to have a very definite opinion of her. Some people referred to her as *slightly eccentric*. Those less kind used terms like *bananas, crackers,* or *batty*.

One thing was certain, Grandma loved life and lived it to the fullest. Each day brought new challenges . . . and in her case, new personalities.

She stood in front of her 1978 Chrysler Newport waving her hands.

"I think you're being paged," Henry said.

When I built up enough courage to glance toward the curb, my worst fears had been realized. My grandmother was dressed in a skimpy tennis outfit—short skirt, midriff top, and visor. A close look at her skinny, wrinkled legs would leave even the most stout-hearted souls scurrying for the nearest bottle of antacid.

"I'm in the mixed doubles with Bobby Riggs in a few minutes," she shouted. "Come on."

I turned to Henry, whose ear-to-ear grin quickly faded. "Please don't tell anyone what you just saw."

"I never do," he said with a smirk.

I glanced sheepishly at Scarlett. "I'm afraid I have to go."

"Why does this keep happening?" she said. She seemed somewhat irritated. "So when can I talk to you about this?"

"Listen," I said. "We're open for business on Saturday night. Can you come by then?"

"Not without an appointment," Henry said.

"Talk to Henry," I said. "He'll fix you up. See you tomorrow night."

I ran over and hopped into the car as quickly as my legs would carry me. I was okay with Henry seeing some of Grandma's antics now and then, but I was sorry Scarlett had to witness it. I waved to both of them as we sped away. Thank goodness it was Friday. Hopefully the weekend would help erase the memory of Grandma's performance in the minds of anyone else who might have been watching. At least I hoped so.

Whether in public or at home behind closed doors, one could never be certain what Grandma had up her sleeve. A Saturday morning breakfast at our house was nothing short of eventful. In fact, had you tried, you probably could have charged admission. The featured attraction? Another of Grandma's escapades. This day was no different.

When I entered the kitchen, I spotted my dad with an expression I could only describe as hopeless. The head of the Collier clan sat at the table with a blood pressure cuff around his neck. Grandma, in a nurse's uniform, prepared to pump up the cuff.

"Mom, I think this is supposed to go around my *arm*," my dad said impatiently.

I squeezed into a chair and smiled weakly at my dad. The show had begun, and I felt fortunate to have a front row seat.

My father peeked at both my mom and me. It was as if he were seeking help, but neither she nor I had any intention of tackling Grandma. My dad wasn't proud of the fact that his mother had controlled his life for years. But how could he be expected to challenge her now? It had been this way since he was young. He had learned to cope, but never to win.

Grandma began pumping up the cuff. I watched as my dad gasped for air.

"Mom!" he choked out. He grabbed his throat. His coloring had taken on a patriotic tone—changing from red to white to blue. His eyes bulged as he looked to me for help.

"Grandma? Don't you think that's enough?" I tried to make the request seem more like a question.

"I s'pose," she said, as she reached for the stethoscope around her neck.

"Mom?" My dad's voice was strained.

"Quiet!" She placed the end of the stethoscope against his neck and listened carefully. Hearing nothing, she stared at the instrument and banged it on the table.

I don't think I had ever seen a senior citizen jump quite that high before. Grandma yanked the stethoscope from her ears and slapped the side of her head. She leaned over and removed the cuff. My dad let out a great sigh and rubbed his neck.

"Let's just eat," he snapped as my mom set a plate of scrambled eggs on the table.

Sensing my dad's displeasure, and fully aware of her mother-in-law's pattern of outrageous behavior, my mom was determined to turn this melodrama into a relaxing family meal.

"So, Charlie, were you surprised to see your grandmother after school yesterday?" she said.

"You might say that." I made a face at my mother. No one wanted to offend Grandma.

"She got back from her Vegas trip a little early, and wanted to help out."

"Thanks a lot," I said, rolling my eyes.

She winked at me and turned to my grandmother. "You must have had a great time, Mom. You look beat."

Grandma abruptly stopped chewing. She wiped her mouth on the sleeve of her nurse's uniform and smiled politely.

"I'm beat 'cause some idiot was banging on my door at three o'clock in the morning."

"At the hotel?" my mom asked.

"No, at the circus! Of course, at the hotel."

"What'd he want?" I asked.

"Oh, he said he thought it was *his* room. Said he must have gotten off on the wrong floor." She reached into the large serving bowl in the center of the table and pulled out a clump of scrambled eggs with her hand. "I'm just glad he wasn't a robber."

I thought to myself for a moment. Something wasn't right here. I couldn't just let this go. "Gram, he *was* a robber."

"What?" she squealed.

"Don't you see? He would never have knocked on the door if it was *his* room. He wanted to find out if someone was in there."

My parents stared at each other, then at me. I could almost read their minds: *He's done it again.*

Grandma slapped my dad on the shoulder. "I hope you realize this boy has quite a gift."

"Yes, Mother, I'm aware of that," my dad said.

It was nice to hear my parents finally acknowledge these powers of mine. Maybe they'd cut me some slack. They might even learn to appreciate these skills. But then, all at once, my dad's attention focused on me.

"Your mother tells me you're taking on clients again."

And suddenly I wished that I had never said anything at all. In every household, a kid needed an ally.

My mother had always been there for me. Why would she betray me this time? I glared at her, then quickly turned away.

"I'm not recruiting them. They find me."

My father was noticeably upset. "Charlie, professional private investigators are licensed by the state," he said. "Where's your license?"

I was well aware that I would not win this battle. But still, it just didn't seem fair. Can you tell a cat not to purr? Can you ask a bird not to sing? It just wasn't natural.

"Aw, let the boy be," my grandma said.

"Mom, please stay out of this," my dad said.

"What's the big deal? He's helping his friends. He's making a little spending money. What's the harm? In my day—"

My dad didn't seem to appreciate Grandma's comments. "But we're not in your day. So, please, let me handle this."

Grandma let out a long sigh.

"Charlie, I asked you a question. Where's your license?" my dad said.

I stared at my plate of eggs and sausage. I decided to say nothing. This was ridiculous. Why would you ask a question you already knew the answer to?

"So you don't have one, huh? Then you don't practice. Understood?"

I gritted my teeth. I was not going to give him the satisfaction of a response.

"Charlie!" my dad roared.

"Okay." I had suddenly lost my appetite. "May I be excused?" I marched to my room and spent the better part of the day curled up with a Sam Solomon novel. In this particular episode, a mysterious redhead was about to get the drop on the master detective. A knock at the door startled me, and I sat up in bed.

"Yeah."

My mom stuck her head in. "Can I come in?"

Was this the same woman who had ratted me out? I was in no mood for an apology. My mother entered the room and immediately noticed my reading material.

"Aren't you tired of"—and then in dramatic fashion—"Sam Solomon, Private Eye?"

"No," I said, without making eye contact.

She paused, then sighed. "Can I talk to you for a minute?"

Oh no. This couldn't be good. I had a bad feeling she was about to ground me for taking on clients again. And if that happened to be my sentence, then so be it. I had survived worse. And I would maintain my cool through it all. I wasn't about to give her the satisfaction of seeing me squirm. Go ahead, Mom, take your best shot.

"What'd you want to talk about?" I said. And then just as the words had trickled off my tongue, I felt this sinking feeling in my chest. What if she had something else in mind—something far worse? My folks were headed to my cousin's wedding tonight, and I was about to have the whole house to myself. What if she felt that she couldn't trust me? What if she wanted to hire a baby-sitter? Oh no. I couldn't take that. I had to do something. I had to take charge. I had to control the conversation—keep it on my terms. I decided to test her. Yeah, that would work. I sat up and smiled.

"Okay, Mom, where does Sam Solomon hide his can of sneezing powder?"

"His what?"

"His sneezing powder."

"Why in the world would he need that?"

"Mom, I'll have you know that if you toss a little sneezing powder into the face of an unsuspecting enemy, you can buy yourself enough time to get out of a tough scrape. Sam's done it dozens of times."

She sighed again. "I have no idea where he keeps it."

"In a secret compartment under his desk."

My mother reached over and slid the book from my hands. She examined it.

"With all those hours you spend at the library, you mean to tell me you can't find something else to read? What do you do there anyway? Not counting the time you're visiting with Eugene, that is."

My mom was referring to Eugene Patterson. Eugene was the library's oldest volunteer. Besides yours truly, he was probably more familiar with routine aspects of

Sam Solomon's life than anyone I'd ever known—not counting my grandfather, of course. Like me, Eugene had not just read about the world's greatest detective, he had studied him. He and I would always play this little game. We'd quiz each other on Sam Solomon trivia. It usually ended in a draw.

"Charlie, I'd like you to do a favor for me," my mom said. "The next time you're at the library, I want you to start reading one of the classics. Can you do that?"

"But, Mom, Sam Solomon *is* a classic. Gramps always thought so. It's challenging, thought provoking . . . and helps sharpen my powers of deduction."

"You have all the answers, don't you?"

I grinned and raised my eyebrows. I had managed to land on my feet once again.

My mom kissed me on the forehead and glanced at her watch. "I'd better get ready. We leave in a little while. I just want to make certain—are you sure you're going to be all right by yourself tonight?"

Be all right? I'd been waiting for this day for months.

"I'll be fine. You go have a good time."

She smiled and scurried out. I grabbed my Sam Solomon hardcover and gazed at the drawing of Sam on the cover. He seemed to be returning the stare.

"What do you think, Sam? Maybe, tonight's the night"—I scooted to the window and looked out at the garage—"when the big score walks right through that door."

CHAPTER 3

The Going for Baroque Caper

A few hours later, I found myself in the living room staring at the TV. There was nothing much of interest to watch. I was just killing time waiting for my parents to leave for the night. I flipped through the channels until a story on the news caught my eye.

"Authorities in suburban Oak Grove are reporting complaints from businesses and homeowners of missing birds in the area. The missing birds range from home pets like cockatoos, conures, and macaws, to the more exotic species of parrots—the eclectus, pionus, quaker, and senegal varieties. Even the local wildlife sanctuary has been unable to locate one of its red-tailed hawks, and this is after having reported last week that one of their falcons is still missing. Authorities are investigating. In other news . . ."

I turned off the set and thought to myself. Something strange was happening—but what? This was the second time that someone had made reference to missing birds recently. Mrs. Jansen had said something in class yesterday. It sounded like the police were looking into it. What I wouldn't give for a chance to tackle a caper like that.

Just then my mom appeared. "Charlie, help me with this." She was wearing a black, floor-length gown. She apparently was having trouble fastening a necklace. "I'm expecting your dad to honk the horn any minute now." And then right on cue—*beep beep!* Dad and Gram were waiting in the minivan in front of the house. Mom was always running late. I quickly fixed the necklace and walked out onto the front porch with her. She leaned over and kissed me on the cheek. I groaned.

There should be rules for parents, not just children. Once you reach the age of twelve, no family member should be able to kiss you in public. It's that simple. Okay, maybe in the house, on your birthday, but for Pete's sake, the front porch is completely off-limits.

"You know our cell phone numbers, and there's dinner in the fridge. We'll be back around eleven," my mom said. She paused and placed her hand on the side of my face. "Are you sure you'll be okay, honey? I just don't feel right leaving you home alone like this."

"I'll be fine."

My grandmother stuck her head out the car window. "Are we finished here?!" She glanced at her watch. She was in a hurry—and let it be known. "I don't want to miss the open bar."

My mother grinned at me. Grandma was amusing, when she didn't have a blood pressure cuff around your neck.

"Okay, be good. I love you." She walked to the car and got in.

I waited on the porch until the van was safely out of sight.

From behind the bushes on the far side of the house emerged Henry, holding a notebook. "Boy, I thought they'd never leave."

"This is gonna be great," I said.

"Hey, did I hear your mom say that they won't be back till eleven?"

I nodded with an ear-to-ear grin.

Henry raised his arms into the air. "Yessss!"

"So, what do you think?" I asked. "Could it happen tonight? Could someone walk into the garage and present us with the caper of capers? The big score? The case we've been waiting for all our lives?"

"Oh yeah." But I knew Henry was just telling me what I wanted to hear. "Tonight's the night for sure."

We hustled to the garage. It had never looked better. A half-dozen lawn chairs filled the space, and a chaise lounge was parked just outside the door. It would make a nice waiting area. We were anticipating a big crowd. Henry had spent the last few days spreading the word to fellow classmates that we would be open for business tonight.

We made a few last-minute alterations to the office décor and finished up just in time. As we stood there and admired our handiwork, there was a knock at the door. I winked at my partner.

"It's showtime," I announced.

As I stuffed myself into my seat, Henry casually strolled to the door and swung it open. With a shaven head and a basketball under his arm, Danny Reardon stood on the other side.

Danny was slightly smarter than your typical jock, but he had chosen sports history over academics. He was a student of the game Dr. Naismith had invented, which is to say basketball. Danny could tell you every NBA championship team beginning with the 1947 Philadelphia Warriors, but could supply little else from his history textbook.

The six-foot-two string bean ducked down as he passed through the doorway. He smiled when he caught sight of my hat.

"Hi, guys," he said, waiting for an invitation to sit down.

Henry glanced at his notebook. "Hi, Dan." Henry escorted him to a chair opposite mine.

"So, what can we do for you?" I asked.

"Well, my next-door neighbor hates it when we play basketball."

"What do you mean?" I said as I folded my hands on the card table.

"My driveway is right next to his yard. And we have a

basketball net over the garage." Danny paused as I took notes on a legal pad.

"Go on," I instructed.

"Well, a lot of times the ball goes in his yard. And it's hard to get 'cause he's got this big dog, you know. I mean sometimes we can get it 'cause the dog's tied to a tree. But sometimes we can't 'cause it's too close to him, and he's not too friendly . . . the dog, that is."

"Do you ever ask your neighbor to get the ball for you?"

"Not anymore. He says if it goes in his yard one more time, he's keepin' it."

I stood and began pacing. I picked up the legal pad and studied my notes. "You say the dog's tied to a tree?"

"Yeah, they nailed this big hook in the tree and attached a long chain to it." Danny stretched his legs out in front of him.

"And what does the dog do when you go in the yard?"

"Well, he's not too happy to see us, I'll tell you that. And there's no way to sneak up on him. He follows you everywhere."

I sat back down and began to sketch a picture on the top page of the pad. I studied it. Redrew it. Analyzed it. Then I smiled.

"Okay, my friend, listen up. The next time the ball goes in that yard and you can't get to it, I want you to—"

Henry cleared his throat, interrupting us. He pointed to a jar filled with dollar bills and coins on one of the workbench shelves.

Danny opened his hand and grinned. Four shiny quarters rested in the center of his palm.

"Just checking," Henry said with a smile.

"Okay now, the ball's in the yard, right?" I said.

"Right."

"I want you to go into the yard and stay close to the fence where the dog can't get at you. Then I want you to walk all the way around the yard . . . once, twice, three times . . . whatever it takes."

"I don't get it."

"Well, the dog's tied up to the tree. When you walk, he'll follow you. The chain will start to wrap around the tree and get shorter and shorter and shorter. Then go pick up the ball." I leaned back in the lawn chair and waited for his reaction.

Danny nodded his head and grinned. "Sweet. Thanks, guys." He got up, dropped his quarters in the jar, and left.

For the next hour, Henry and I engaged in a relaxing game of English darts while waiting for our next client. *Relaxing*, however, might not be the way Henry would have described the experience.

"*Double* in?" Henry whined. "Why do we always have to double in?"

"Because those are the rules. Why would you want to play any other way?"

"So we're not here all night. I'll never get it in one of those little holes."

"We either play the game the right way, or we don't play at all," I said. "For your information, in Episode #8—*The Going for Baroque Caper*—Sam Solomon, while interviewing a new assistant, clearly states that breaking the rules is like breaking your word. And a responsible and ethical private eye would never—"

"Yeah, yeah, yeah. I betcha Sam wasn't playin' darts when he came up with that one."

A light knock at the door interrupted our friendly spat.

"Who's next?" I asked.

Henry looked around for the legal pad. "Where is it?" he said impatiently.

"It was right here a minute ago," I said.

"You know, if we had a computer in here like normal people, we'd have all this stuff stored in a nice database, and we wouldn't be running around looking for a pad of paper like a couple of dopes."

Someone was now pounding on the door.

"Sam Solomon didn't need a computer to keep track of his clients. And we don't either," I said.

Henry shook his head disgustedly and swung open the door. Standing in the entryway with a parrot sitting on her shoulder was Jessica Pearson. The sixth-grader didn't wait to be asked in as she brushed by Henry and sat down.

"Let's go, boys, we're on the clock."

Jessica was all business. She controlled all situations

and won all arguments. In a conversation with Jessica, you were always the listener. And she wasn't afraid to point out your shortcomings.

"I'm on a tight schedule tonight."

I glared at Henry. I couldn't believe my best friend would do this to me. Why had he booked Jessica? After all, this was the office of Charlie Collier, Snoop for Hire. *I* called the shots here. I didn't have to work under these conditions.

Jessica slammed her fist on the card table, nearly collapsing it. "If you think I'm going to just sit here . . ."

"It's nice to see you again, Jessica," I said. Killer kindness was always the way to tame a restless client.

Jessica rolled her eyes. She wasn't buying it. "Cut it out, Collier. I got a problem. You wanna help me or not?"

I sat down and reflected. I had taken on difficult clients before. And although Jessica was certain to test my patience, I needed to maintain my professionalism.

"Okay, let's have it," I said.

Jessica held her fist up to her shoulder, and Merlin, the parrot, climbed on. She set him on the table.

"I bought this parrot about a week ago from Bird World over at the mall. I wanted a talking parrot, and I told the salesman that. He guaranteed that this bird would repeat every word it hears. But watch . . ."

She stroked the top of the parrot's head and leaned over.

"Merlin, say, 'Good evening, Queen Jessica.'"

The bird remained silent. Henry glanced at me. He mouthed *Queen Jessica* and tried to keep from laughing.

"See . . . nothing," she moaned.

I reached over to the bird and extended my hand, then quickly pulled it back. Better to get permission first.

"May I?"

Jessica nodded. Merlin climbed onto my hand. I examined the creature closely. I held him up to my ear and listened, then set the bird back down on the table.

"Hmmm, did you go back to the pet store and complain?"

"Of course, Einstein. And the salesman told me the same thing: 'This bird will repeat whatever he hears.'"

"Maybe you should—," Henry started to add, but was quickly cut off.

"I don't need analysis from a second banana. I came to talk to him," she said, pointing at me.

Henry smiled politely and sat down. I could see he was about to explode.

"Listen, Collier, I want you to go down to the pet shop and investigate this guy. Get me some dirt on him."

"I don't think we'll have to."

"What do you mean?" she asked.

I stood up and walked around the table so that Merlin's back was to me. I leaned over and clapped my hands loudly. Jessica and Henry both jumped. The parrot, however, had not moved a feather.

"What was that for?" she grumbled.

"The salesman was right. This bird *will* repeat whatever it hears."

"What are you saying?"

"I'm afraid your bird is deaf."

Henry popped up from his chair, grabbed the money jar, and extended it to Jessica for payment. She pulled several coins from her pocket and jammed them into the jar.

"Hey, Jessica," I said. "You'd better keep an eye on Merlin. A lot of pet birds have been disappearing from around here. It's all over the news."

She apparently did not appreciate the warning. She threw open the door and left in a huff.

"That poor bird," Henry said, shaking his head.

"Poor bird? He's the lucky one," I said.

"What do you mean?"

I pulled the fedora down over my eyes and smiled. "*He* doesn't have to listen to her."

After having survived Jessica, and a half-dozen other clients with problems ranging from mysterious, unsigned love letters to booby-trapped rolls of toilet paper in the girls' bathroom, we both decided we had earned a well-deserved dinner break. We ordered an extra-large pizza and feasted on it while waiting for our next client. In less than ten minutes, the empty pizza box rested on the card table.

"I'm gonna puke right here," Henry moaned.

"You do, and you'll have to clean it up," I said as I climbed to my feet. I pointed at the last piece of pizza. "It's all yours."

"Are you kidding?"

"Well, somebody has to," I said.

"Just where is it written that you *have* to finish a pizza?! I mean, what's the big deal?"

"There is a pizza code of honor. You order it, you eat it. End of discussion."

Henry took a deep breath, peeled the last piece of pizza off the bottom of the cardboard box, folded it into fours, closed his eyes, and jammed it into his mouth.

"I just realized something," I said.

"What?"

"Scarlett never showed up. I wonder what happened."

"Beats me," Henry said as he swallowed the last bite of pizza. "We don't need her business anyway." He glanced at his watch. "It's almost eleven. We'd better get this place cleaned up. Your parents will be here any minute."

I shrugged. "You know something, Henry?"

"What?"

"I'm numb. I don't feel a thing."

"Huh? What are you talking about?" Henry asked

as he started folding up the lawn chairs and putting them away.

"This whole *Snoop for Hire* business. It's just not as exciting as it used to be."

"You want exciting? Check the jar. We made some decent money tonight."

"No, I mean that none of these cases were very challenging. We solved every one from right here in the garage."

"What's boring about that? No legwork."

"That's no fun. I enjoy the hunt. Tracking down leads . . . questioning sources . . . going undercover."

Henry picked up the card table and began breaking it down. "Charlie, our clients are other sixth-graders. They don't have the kinds of problems you're talking about. These aren't Sam Solomon cases." He slid the card table behind an extension ladder. "You're just gonna have to get used to figuring out brain busters and solving meaningless problems for kids at school." Henry folded up one of the lawn chairs and lifted it onto a hook on the far wall. "Face it, nobody in his right mind is going to hire a twelve-year-old kid to solve a real mystery."

"Well, I don't see why—" I froze in mid-sentence. Headlights beamed through the garage window. "Oh no, my parents."

As the overhead garage door began to rise, Henry

and I slipped out the side door and crouched down behind a row of bushes.

As the van pulled up the driveway, half of Grandma's body extended out the sunroof. She was wearing a ten-gallon cowboy hat and was swinging a lasso over her head.

"Will you sit down, Mom, before you lose your head?" my dad yelled.

"Not till I catch that pesky varmint." Grandma swung the rope over her head, tossed it at the garbage cans, and actually snared one. The painful sound of metal hitting metal soon followed as the can banged against the side of the van. And if that wasn't bad enough, my dad ran over the can, smashing it beneath the van's rear tires.

"C'mon, let's sneak back into the house," I whispered.

Henry started to snicker. "No offense, man, but your granny is hilarious."

Over the years, I had heard much stronger language regarding my grandmother's mental fitness. Even my parents were at odds at what to do with her. It's not that my mom wasn't fond of her mother-in-law; it was just that her strange behavior was so unpredictable, it made it difficult to run a household.

More than once, Mom had asked my dad to consider placing his mother in what they would refer to as "an assisted-living facility." But Dad would always cave. I wasn't sure if his response was the action of a loving and caring son, or someone who feared this slightly unstable senior citizen.

I, however, had my own theory. Unlike others, I firmly believed that my grandmother was perfectly sane . . . that she knew exactly what she was doing, and was messing with everyone for fun. As you might guess, I kept that opinion to myself. But the more I thought about it, the more certain I was. After all, who in his right mind wouldn't love to wake up each morning and assume a new identity—one of his own choosing—one filled with excitement and intrigue? This was precisely what Grandma was doing, and I for one was a little jealous.

Henry and I scurried into the house. We grabbed a deck of cards from one of the kitchen drawers, quickly poured two glasses of milk, and sat down at the dinner table. Henry split the deck of cards in half—as if to suggest we were in a heated battle of War.

When my folks and Grandma came in the back door, Henry and I greeted them with two of the most innocent expressions we could muster. My mom smiled at us, and said, "Nice to see you, Henry," while my dad just shook his head. He had other things on his mind.

"Mom, I can't just buff that out," my dad said. "I'm going to have to go to a body shop."

"Oh, quit your bellyaching," Grandma said. "I

bagged us a no-good desperado out there. You oughta be thanking me."

My mom took my dad by the arm and gently steered him out of the room. Over the years Mom had taken on the role of referee in bouts between Dad and Grandma. She was good at it. I almost bought her a black-and-white-striped referee shirt as a little joke for Mother's Day last year, but then dismissed the idea. It's doubtful that my dad would have appreciated the humor.

"Okay, which one of you sidewinders is holding the 'dead man's hand'?" Grandma said as she pulled up a chair and joined us. She placed her cowboy hat on the table and dropped her lasso onto the floor.

"Huh?" Henry said.

"The 'dead man's hand,'" Gram said. "You know, aces and eights. The cards Wild Bill Hickok was holding when he met his untimely demise."

I smiled. "Oh . . . well, we're playing War not poker."

"Ahh, that game's for tenderfoots. Gimme those cards."

My mom poked her head in. "Henry, how are you getting home?"

"I have to call my dad," he said.

"Don't bother. I'll take you. Let me change first," she said as she ducked out.

"Okay, gentlemen," Grandma said as she finished shuffling. "The game is seven-card stud, deuces wild.

Ante up or make room for the next player." She winked and began dealing.

Henry leaned over to me and whispered, "I love her, man."

I smiled. *Me too*, I thought.

CHAPTER 4

The Loss of Patients Caper

Maybe it was because it was a Monday. Everything seemed to move in slow motion. I watched the second hand creep ever so slowly on a large, round clock on the front wall above Mrs. Jansen's head. Whoever said that time stands still when you stare at a clock could not have been more correct. Only four days remained before spring break, and I was oh so ready. I had hoped that the time off would help me regain a desire to solve even the simplest mysteries. Henry and I hadn't booked any new clients. Maybe they sensed that I was losing interest in their problems, that I longed for something more, that I was ready for the next challenge.

Henry was right. No adult would ever hire a kid to solve a real case. I was destined to be, at best, a detective wannabe. The clock read 2:29. One more minute. The second hand seemed to crawl as it climbed toward its target. Then, finally . . . *RRRRING!* As the classroom came alive again, I stuffed books into my backpack and got up to leave. That's when Scarlett Alexander stopped next to my desk.

"I still need to talk to you—unless you're too busy," she said disgustedly.

"What do you mean? You were the one who didn't show up on Saturday."

"What are you talking about?" she snapped. "I wanted to come but Henry told me there weren't any more openings. He said all the appointments were filled."

"What? We had plenty of openings."

Scarlett placed her hands on her hips and scowled. She scanned the room. She had to be looking for Henry. And he must have anticipated that because he was nowhere in sight.

"I'm sorry about all of this," I said. "What about right now? Do you have time?"

"My mom's picking me up," she said. "We're headed to the library. But I suppose I've got a couple of minutes."

"Okay, great, so what can I do for you?"

"Well, not really me—it's for my grandpa."

Her grandpa? Did I hear her right? An *adult* actually needed *my* help? Could this be it? Could this be the assignment I had been waiting for all my life? I was starting to hyperventilate. I needed to relax. I needed to make Scarlett think that I handled cases for grown-ups all the time.

"Oh, I remember now," I said. "Some*one* or some-*thing* is missing, right?"

"Uh-huh. His parrot, Socrates, is gone."

Wait a minute. A missing parrot? This was just like the story on the news the other day. This was a big deal. And she wanted *me* to help? I couldn't believe it.

But before she could continue, Sherman Doyle slipped in between us, shielding Scarlett from my view. He stood there and stared at me.

"Is there something I can do for you, Sherman?"

He just glared. What was this guy doing? Granted, Sherman was no one to be taken lightly but Scarlett was in need, and at that moment he really didn't scare me. I tried to look around him, but the man-child was a wall unto himself. I prayed that this interruption wouldn't discourage Scarlett, but when I stood up on my chair and peered over Sherman, she was gone. Darn it!

I sneered at the big oaf. He was messing with my big case. He'd better have a good reason.

"So, what do you want?" I said impatiently.

"You been real quiet in here lately. Just keep it that way." He flashed a dumb smile, and was off.

That was it. *That* was all he wanted. *That* was the reason I lost an opportunity to take on the biggest case of my life. I had a good notion to follow him out to the playground and . . . Yeah, right. Like I would ever confront someone like that. I began to recall the stories

I had heard about how Sherman had supposedly dismembered kids at his former school. No one had ever spoken to his victims . . . either because they didn't exist, or because they were no longer of this earth. I didn't care to find out.

I slung my backpack over my shoulder and ran outside to look for Scarlett. I first surveyed the playground. Not there. I checked the parking lot. Another dead end. I had to find her. I had to tell her that I'd be more than happy to take on her case. I continued searching for the next several minutes. It was as if she had vanished into thin air.

Then I spotted Henry at the bus stop. I ran over to confront him. "Thanks a lot, pal," I said.

"What's wrong with you?" he said.

"You told Scarlett we were all booked up on Saturday night? What was that about? We had plenty of openings."

"Charlie, relax. I just wanted to keep a few slots open for walk-ins. That's all."

"Well, I gotta find her and straighten things out."

"It's too late for that now," Henry said.

"What do you mean?"

"I saw her mom pick her up a minute ago."

"That's just great," I said. It wasn't bad enough that I lost a chance to spend some quality time with Scarlett. Now it appeared that I had let a killer case slip right through my fingers. How could I fix this? And then I remembered. Scarlett had said something about going over to the library. If I hustled I might be able to catch her there. Then I could finally clear up this whole matter. "I'll see you later," I said to Henry.

"Where you headed? You're not taking the bus?"

"No, I gotta be somewhere."

"Want some company?" Henry asked.

I didn't want to offend him but I knew that it would be much tougher to patch things up with Scarlett with Henry around.

"No, thanks. I'll see you tomorrow."

Twenty minutes later I entered the library. Scarlett had to be here somewhere. She just had to. I began a thorough search of the entire building. I strolled up and down each aisle, poked my head into every room, even went outside and checked the parking lot for her car. After ten minutes or so, I was fairly certain that I had missed her. Either she had already come and gone, or she had never been here in the first place.

I was beginning to worry that I had missed my chance of landing a Sam Solomon–type of case. Scarlett had to be getting frustrated with our inability to sit down and talk this out. She might even think that I wasn't interested in helping her. Henry hadn't done me any favors by turning her away the other night. I wouldn't be surprised if she sought out another private eye, although I didn't know any other twelve-year-olds with their own agencies.

At that point there was little else to do but go home and lick my wounds. I was starting to feel sorry for myself—losing a shot at the big score and all. But then a better idea popped into my head. I suddenly thought of the perfect remedy for the blues. I decided to head to the library basement and immerse myself in a Sam Solomon mystery.

The lighting in the lower level was dim at best. It was as if you were reading through a haze. But in the basement, you could cuddle up with a friend—on paper that is—and imagine you were a swashbuckler, a titan, a crusader, a desperado, or a 1930s private cop. I sat down in a chair in the farthest corner from the staircase, surrounded by walls of words.

That particular day was no different. I pictured myself alongside Sam, ready to assist him in whatever predicament lay before him. In Episode #3—*The Loss of Patients Caper*—Sam had been hired to locate a dozen people who, after having been admitted to a local hospital for routine surgeries, suddenly disappeared. It was one of my favorites. I had read it before, countless times. But like watching a favorite film, I never grew tired of this character. And even when I knew who was lurking around a dark corner, it didn't matter. I still felt the rush.

I sometimes wonder what my life would have been like if I had never encountered Sam Solomon. Fortunately, I'll never have to worry about that—thanks to my grandfather. It was Grandpa Jim, Gram's better half, who introduced me to Sam Solomon. They were Gramps's favorite books when he was a kid—and now they're mine. I still miss him. I can't believe it's been more than five years since he died. Grandma took it pretty hard at first, but then like a real trouper, she pulled it together and continued on with life—in her own crazy sort of way.

I looked up as a door opened on the far basement wall and out stepped Eugene Patterson. He always volunteered at the library in the afternoons. He pushed a handcart in my direction and smiled when he saw me. It was at the same moment that Eugene attempted to turn his cart at too sharp an angle.

"Oh no!" he said as a pile of books fell onto the floor.

I jumped from my chair. "Need some help, Eugene?"

The old man scratched his head, confused. "Not sure how that happened."

I knelt down to help retrieve the fallen books.

"Thanks, Charlie."

As I returned each book to the cart, I noticed that many were in poor condition. "These look pretty old."

"They are. A lot of them are first editions."

"So, what are you going to do with them?" I said.

"Oh, they're headed to the archives. Too valuable to sit on the shelves."

I slid the last of the books onto Eugene's cart.

"Well, thanks a lot, Charlie. I'd better be on my way."

"You're welcome." I watched Eugene slowly trudge down the aisle—then he stopped suddenly.

"Hey, didn't you forget something?" he said.

I looked at him, confused. "What?"

"Sam Solomon trivia. Come on. Try to stump me."

"Oh yeah," I said, smiling. I thought hard for a moment. I needed an especially challenging Sam Solomon tidbit. I closed my eyes tightly and tried to think. But the more I tried, the less I could come up with. Nothing was happening. "Umm," I said, stalling. I let out a nervous laugh. What was wrong with me? This Scarlett thing had messed me up big-time. I couldn't think straight. This was not difficult stuff. After about thirty seconds, I decided to just spit out anything.

"How did Sam escape from his office when the Hudson Gang was trying to break in?"

Eugene just shook his head. "The rope ladder hidden in the flower box." He seemed disappointed. "You asked me that one last week."

"Oh yeah. Sorry."

"Aw, don't worry about it. Just be sure to think up a new one next time. A real good one."

"I'll work on it."

Eugene glanced at his watch. "Appears my sentence is almost up for the day. See you tomorrow," he said as he dragged his cart to the archives.

I fell back into my chair with my book, but minutes later, I sat up. I just couldn't concentrate. What was wrong with me? If I could no longer become engrossed in one of Sam's mysteries, then what was left? The future seemed bleak at best. I was beginning to feel sorry for myself. This was worse than I thought. I had to get out of this funk. You're Charlie Collier, Snoop for Hire, for Pete's sake, I told myself. Snap out of it.

I reopened the Sam Solomon novel and forced myself to concentrate. But it was no use. I kept thinking about Scarlett. It would be so great to work for her on a real case. I began to worry that it might never happen though. I had to make this right. I just had to. But how? What I needed to do was to sit down and talk with her, and to officially take on this case. I decided not to wait until school tomorrow. I needed to take action right now. I'd go over to her house. That was what I'd do.

The thought of showing up on Scarlett's front porch made me a little nervous. I had never done anything like that before. I had walked by her house any number of times, just hoping that she might see me and ask me in. Yeah, like that was ever going to happen. But actually going over there—and ringing the doorbell, no less—now, this was a big step. She might not be too crazy about me just showing up uninvited. This whole thing could backfire. But what did I have to lose anyway? It was worth a shot, right? I decided to risk it.

On the walk to Scarlett's house, I tried to prepare myself for the worst. If things didn't go well, and I blew a chance for a shot at the big score, then so be it. I tried to convince myself that there would be other opportunities. I suppose I might stumble onto the ultimate case one of these days. For years I dreamed of a client . . . a mysterious redhead . . . yeah . . . walking into the garage and requesting my services. It was just like in *The Loss of Patients Caper:* The daughter of one of the missing patients hires Sam to locate her father. I can just imagine the same thing happening to me. She'd be gorgeous . . . and fragile . . . very fragile . . . and distressed. Her life would be in jeopardy. She would have exhausted all other means. I would be her last resort. I let out a sigh. Now that would be outstanding.

I suppose I would have relived that image multiple times had not the rattle of a transmission and a blaring car horn startled me. It was the familiar sound of Grandma's oversize Chrysler Newport. The boat screeched to a halt, jumping up onto the curb. Grandma popped out. She was wearing an orange jumpsuit—the prison variety. I smiled. This was a new look. I didn't dare ask about it.

"Hop in. I'll give you a ride," Grandma said.

Now, I appreciated her offer, but I'd just as soon have reworked that daydream. The redhead was waiting for me.

"Thanks, Gram, but I'll pass."

"It wasn't a question. It was an order. Get in," she said. Her tone was deadly serious.

I looked at her funny, but I didn't argue. I threw my backpack onto the rear seat and slid in. Was something wrong at home?

"What's going—," I started to say, but Gram held up her hand.

"No talking. Just sit."

I sat back in my seat. Chalk up another failed attempt to connect with Scarlett. But, who knew, maybe Gram was doing me a favor. Maybe showing up at Scarlett's house unannounced would have been a bad idea.

I didn't say a word as we whisked through town, ten to fifteen miles over the speed limit at all times. Grandma was a relatively safe driver, but she had the need for speed. It made my dad crazy sometimes. He had finally refused to ride with her. I, on the other hand, enjoyed it. After all, in my line of work, high-speed chases were commonplace. I had better get accustomed to them.

When we turned onto Briar Avenue, the old Oak Grove City Hall building came into view. I knew at that point that we weren't headed home. I wanted to know where we were going but thought it best to wait until Gram was ready to reveal our official destination. Her eyes were fixed on the road. The farther we drove, the less familiar I was with the surroundings. I couldn't keep quiet any longer. I had to know.

"Gram, where exactly . . . ?"

Without turning her head, Grandma made herself very clear. "No questions. Just sit there. You might learn something."

We soon entered an old section of town. I noticed an army surplus store on one of the corners as we passed by. The buildings weren't necessarily run-down . . . just old. It was the kind of place where you'd never find a mall, just a series of mom-and-pop shops up and down the main street. Most of the buildings had to be at least seventy-five years old. They did have character though.

Grandma turned the corner at Kendall Avenue and stopped the car in front of an old barber shop . . . the kind with the red-and-white pole that spins around. On the front door were metal numbers that read 3116. She opened the driver's door and nodded for me to follow. We both got out of the car and walked past the front window. I could see several older men in chairs waiting for haircuts. Then Gram looked around, as if she didn't want anyone to see where we were headed. It was then that I felt a twinge in my gut. The same feeling I would get sometimes when reading a Sam Solomon novel, right before Sam gets himself into a jam. I loved the sensation.

I followed my grandmother along the side of the building to its rear. We stopped at the back door. It was unlocked, and Grandma pulled it open. We made our way up a set of creaky wooden stairs. When we reached the landing, Grandma nodded at an unmarked door at the end of the hallway. She led the way. As we approached the doorway, she looked over her shoulder at me. I detected a half smile. It was the first friendly signal I had gotten from her in the last thirty minutes. She proceeded to knock twice, then scraped her fingernails on the face of the door and knocked three more times. It was clearly some sort of password. But what was on the other side of this door? Where had she taken me? Why all the mystery?

I could faintly make out an oddly familiar voice from the other side. "Come in," he said.

Grandma was now sporting a full grin. It was the type of facial expression that people have when they can't wait to see the look on your face. Like your mother on Christmas morning as you unwrap the best gift. She stepped back and motioned for me to open the door. I was a little fearful of what was waiting for me on the other side, but I didn't want her to sense my nervousness.

I turned the knob and pushed. The door was stuck. Not surprising given the age and appearance of this place. I tried it a second time . . . nothing. I glanced at my grandmother. She shook her head and threw a shoulder into the door. It opened right up. She stepped back, allowing me to enter first. I took a deep breath and poked my head inside.

CHAPTER 5

The Steamed Carats Caper

The room was dimly lit. I'm not quite certain what I was expecting but this was nothing special, that was for sure. I stepped in for a better look. Grandma followed, closing the door behind us. I examined the surroundings. We were in a dingy, under-sized office. The plaster walls were cracked and stained. The window . . . there was only one . . . was partially shattered with a tiny hole still visible. Looked almost like a bullet hole . . . a .38 if I had to guess. There were no rugs or curtains. The only light came from a lamp flickering on the desk. There was a tall leather chair with its back to us pushed up against the desk. A picture of Franklin Delano Roosevelt hung on the far wall, with a wooden file cabinet just beneath it. Hanging from a hook on the wall was a wrinkled trench coat and a black fedora. There was an old, moth-eaten couch and a three-legged table filled with papers next to the window, and that was about it. But something about it felt familiar and comforting.

I turned to Gram. "I don't get it. Why are we here?"

"I'm a little disappointed in you, Charlie. Take a really good look around."

I reexamined the contents of the room. Was I supposed to recognize this place or something? And then it hit me. Of course. I smiled. Actually, I beamed, and my grandmother could sense my delight. The bullet hole in the window. The three-legged table. The portrait of FDR. And the unmistakable fedora and trench coat. On the surface, this space just appeared to be a sorry excuse for an office. But upon closer examination, it was an exact replica of Sam Solomon's office in 1938 Chicago. Just as I had pictured it. It was almost as if I were reading about it for the first time—like I did in Episode #1—*The Steamed Carats Caper.*

"I knew you'd recognize it," Grandma said.

All at once the desk chair spun around, and seated before me was a gentleman I would never have expected to have found there. "Eugene Patterson?" I said, looking at him quizzically. The volunteer from the library? Now I was even more confused. What was Eugene doing here? And what was this office all about? It was fantastic. But who had put it all together, and why?

"Welcome, Charlie," Eugene said. He motioned for me to join him.

I looked at my grandmother. It wasn't as though I was asking for permission. I just wanted to make sure she was okay with all of this.

"Well, go ahead," she said.

I continued to soak in all the wonderment of this incredible place as I sat down across from Eugene. "I don't understand," I mumbled.

With a smug look, the old man sat back in his chair and crossed his arms. Grandma was now sitting on the old, ratty couch. Both of them were staring at me, silently, waiting for my reaction to all of this. I was dying to know what was going on. After about thirty seconds, curiosity forced my hand.

I jumped up. "What is all this?"

Eugene and Grandma laughed.

"This is my office, Charlie. What did you think it was?" Eugene said.

I didn't know what to make of it. Why exactly would Eugene have an office? I thought he was retired. What was going on here?

"Your office? What kind of office?"

"Well, you should know that. We're both in the same line of work."

I narrowed my eyes. "This is a detective agency? You run a detective agency?

Eugene nodded.

"But I thought you were just a volunteer at the library."

"That's my cover," Eugene said. "You know, the library is a great resource when you're researching a case. Heck, most people think I'm just another senior citizen trying to kill time and waiting for the call from upstairs. And that's fine with me."

I looked around the room. "How long have you been doing all of this?"

Grandma laughed. "A long time," she said. "How long's it been, Eugene . . . fifty-plus years now since we set up shop?"

I stared at my grandmother. "We?"

"We," Eugene said. "You didn't know your grandmother once worked in a detective agency, did you?"

"Are you kidding, Gram? Why didn't you ever tell me? You know I love this stuff."

"It was best to be discreet," she said. "You know what that word means, don't you?"

I nodded.

"When you spend most of your life undercover, you learn not to advertise it," she said.

"Wait a minute. I thought you were a switchboard operator."

"Well, I was . . . during the war."

"And that's not all she did in W-W-Two," Eugene said.

"What do you mean?" I asked. My grandmother seemed slightly embarrassed.

"Tell the boy, Constance."

She rose from the couch and walked over to the desk. Pausing, she turned toward me with intense seriousness, and said, "This information can't leave this room."

I nodded. Gram didn't have to worry about me spilling the beans. In all my years as a private eye, I had never betrayed a client. Confidentiality was required in our profession, and I respected that.

"During the Second World War, while I worked at the telephone company, I was approached by a young, good-looking lieutenant in Naval Intelligence." She winked at Eugene.

"Eugene?" I said.

Eugene smiled, and pointed his finger at me. "That's classified too, young man."

"Don't worry," I assured him. I turned to my grandmother. "Well?"

"When I was young, Charlie, I was a lot like you. I loved to solve things—crossword puzzles, word jumbles, anything with letters—and a lot of people knew I had this little skill."

"Don't be modest," Eugene said. "It wasn't so little."

"You see, when you run a switchboard," Grandma continued, "you have access to a lot of communications from all over the country . . . from all over the world for that matter. And our intelligence forces were worried that enemy sympathizers, here in the U.S., were in contact with their cohorts overseas. Our military would try to intercept their telephone conversations. And since I was an overseas operator, many of those calls had to come through me. But it wasn't so easy because they were always in code."

"Code?" I said.

"That's right," Gram said.

"It was your grandma's job to decode those messages for us." Eugene grinned. "And there was none better."

"I can't believe all this. Gram, you were a hero. You too, Eugene."

"Just doin' our jobs," Eugene said humbly.

"That's how it was back then," Grandma said. "You did whatever your country asked you to do, you didn't ask questions, and you didn't look for a pat on the back."

"So, how did you get *here*?"

"When the war ended, there weren't many opportunities to put my skills to good use," Gram said. "Nobody was hiring cryptologists."

"You were a cryptologist?" I asked.

Grandma looked embarrassed.

But Eugene grinned. "She was the best we had. There wasn't a code she couldn't crack."

"It was quite a ride," Grandma said.

"But what happened after the war?" I asked. "Did you keep working for the government?"

"No, I returned to the switchboard," she said. "But

it wasn't nearly as exciting. And then a few months later, Eugene paid me a second visit."

"Best move I ever made," Eugene said.

"He told me that he'd been discharged from the navy and was considering setting up his own detective agency. And he asked me to join him."

"You see, Charlie," Eugene said, "I'd learned a lot during my years as a Naval Intelligence officer. Enough to hang out a shingle and set up my own shop. But I couldn't do it alone." He winked at Gram. "I needed an associate. Someone I could trust. And someone who folks would never suspect was in the detective business. Your grandmother was the perfect choice."

"Gram, How come you never told me about all this? Is this the reason for all your different . . . personalities? Did Grandpa know? Does my dad know?"

"Your grandfather knew. And like a true Sam Solomon fan, he loved all the mystery and intrigue. But your dad, on the other hand, knows nothing about this. And that's just the way I want to keep it."

"Why?"

"He should think of me as his mother. Period. All that cloak and dagger stuff would only muddy things up."

It was already pretty muddied up, I thought to myself. She was probably right though.

"Then how come you're telling me all this? I mean, don't get me wrong, I'm glad. But why?"

"Because you're different," Gram said. "Because you have a hunger for mystery and intrigue. And because your dad gets on your case all the time about your little business. I thought it might be nice for you to see how a real detective agency operates."

"And today at the library," Eugene said, "I couldn't help but notice that you seemed restless. Like something was wrong. I've never known you to have a hard time thinking up a Sam Solomon trivia question before. It just seemed like the right time to lift your spirits a little. And"—Eugene looked at Gram, who nodded—"to make you a little offer."

"An offer?" I said.

Eugene stood up and walked to the far wall. He reached for the fedora and placed it on his head, then he slipped on the trench coat. He returned and sat on the edge of the desk.

"Your grandmother's told me about the detective agency you run out of your garage."

I glanced at Grandma and smiled. She was the only one at home who never gave me grief about my small-business venture.

"Very enterprising," Eugene said. "I applaud you."

"Thanks."

"Is it safe to assume that most of your cases are, shall we say, trivial in nature?"

I nodded.

"How'd you like a taste of the big score? With *real* clients, makin' some *real* money . . ."

"With *real* danger?" I asked.

"Well, it happens occasionally, but we don't wish for it." He took off his hat and flipped it across the room. It hit against the wall and dropped onto the hook. A perfect shot. "If you haven't noticed, Charlie, I'm getting a little up in years. I could use a little help around here."

I was having a hard time believing everything I was hearing. Eugene? A real private detective?

"Charlie, I'd like you to become my apprentice. Learn the ropes. Pay your dues in this business. And maybe someday all of this will be yours."

I knew that I should jump at this opportunity. I'd been itching for some new clients . . . mature clients . . . real clients. But I was hesitant. I mean, who in his right mind is going to hire a ninety-year-old guy solve a case? Heck, it was as unlikely as hiring a twelve-year-old. I just couldn't imagine a mysterious redhead walking through that door and actually requesting Eugene's services. It just wasn't going to happen.

"So, what do you say?" Eugene said. "You can start right away. How about tomorrow after school?"

I had to think this thing out, and quickly. Granted, this wasn't the dream job I had longed for, but maybe I could learn something here. Refine my skills. Even if it just meant listening to Eugene tell stories from his glory days, it might still be interesting. And if this Scarlett thing never panned out, this just might take my mind off of it. And, you know, as unlikely as something really big ever happening here was, there was probably a better chance that a real client with a real problem would wander into this office than into my garage.

I looked at Gram, who smiled and nodded in encouragement. I then turned to the senior private eye. "Eugene, I accept."

He reached out to shake my hand. "It'll be nice having an associate again."

Associate. I liked the way it sounded. I could get used to that.

Eugene sat back in his chair, pulled a candy bar from his pocket, broke off a piece, and was just about to pop it into his mouth when Gram jumped off the couch and grabbed it from him.

"What do you think you're doing?" Gram said.

"I just need a little energy boost, that's all."

"Have you forgotten what your doctor told you?"

"My cholesterol is fine," Eugene said, rolling his eyes.

"Your triglycerides are off the charts." Grandma said. "You got any more of these around here?"

"Not a one," Eugene said.

"All right. Let's keep it that way."

When Grandma turned away from Eugene, the old man made a face at her and winked at me.

"Now, where were we?" Eugene said. "Oh yeah . . . remember, Charlie, not a word to anyone about all this."

"Don't worry," I said. And just as the words slipped off my tongue, I thought about Henry. Not tell Henry? We were partners. How could I cut him out of the action? I'm sure he'd get a kick out of this—if for no other reason than the fact we'd be making some real money.

"Ready to go?" Grandma said.

"Wait. You mean I can't even tell Henry?"

"Not a soul," Eugene said. "Listen, Charlie, let me explain something. This is a *private* private detective agency. By that I mean—I work for a select group of clients. I'm not out there advertising. I don't need any new business. And I have to make sure I'm available when my best and most important client calls—my favorite uncle."

"Uncle?" I said.

"Uncle Sam," Gram whispered.

"I still do some top-secret work for the government. So, you see, it's best if we just keep things between ourselves. You got it?"

"Yes, sir."

"Not to mention the fact that your folks probably wouldn't approve of you joining forces with me. Your grandmother tells me they're not too keen on your little business."

"That's one way to put it," I said.

"So, I'll see you tomorrow after school, okay?" Eugene said. "And, oh, by the way . . ." He opened the top desk drawer and pulled out something. He tossed it across the room to me. It was a key—a skeleton key.

I looked at him curiously. "What's this for?"

"It opens the front door," Eugene said. "But it might also open up a whole lot more."

CHAPTER 6

The Dues and Don'ts Caper

During the drive home, I found myself imagining what might happen. Maybe, just maybe, a legitimate client would stroll into the office with a Sam Solomon brand of mystery. It would be great. Yeah. This just might be the perfect move. I could probably close up the garage for a while. No need to maintain two offices. I wasn't quite sure how I'd break the news to Henry though. It didn't seem right shutting him out, but what choice did I have? My new associate had asked me to keep a lid on our little partnership.

I supposed I could tell Henry that I just needed a little break—that I was worried about burning out. He might just buy it. It wouldn't affect our friendship. I'd see to that. We'd just be closing the book on one chapter of our lives, and opening another. I was fairly certain I could sell it. And then, at the right time, I'd tell him about my association with Eugene. I was sure he'd understand.

I was suddenly jarred back to reality when Grandma maneuvered one of her patented U-turns on the four-lane downtown thoroughfare at the height of rush hour. It certainly got us noticed. The flurry of catcalls never seemed to faze her, though. And why not? A cryptologist in WWII. Undercover private detective assignments. It all made sense to me now.

Suddenly Grandma slammed on the brakes. "Looks like we got a freight train up ahead. We'll be here for a few minutes."

"That's okay. Nothing can spoil today. It's been great. Thanks, Gram."

"I'm glad. I knew you'd flip when you found out about Eugene and me. And you know why?"

I shook my head.

"It's because we're a lot alike, you and me. We both enjoy a good adventure. And if we can't find one, some-times we have to create one for ourselves." She winked. "Know what I mean?"

"Uh-huh."

"But there were times when I didn't have to pretend—when I didn't play make-believe for my own amusement. I can remember many times where I had to assume other identities to help solve a case. It was fun. I enjoyed it." She sighed. "Now it's hard to give it all up."

"I understand."

"You just don't get something like that out of your

system overnight. So, every so often I have a little fun." She leaned over and grinned. "And knowing that it drives your dad crazy makes it even better."

I laughed.

"A lot of people think I'm a little eccentric. Maybe so. But you know what I think—I think they're all jealous. They wish *they* could get away with it."

"I think you may be right."

"So, I want you to really enjoy this time with Eugene. I want you to have adventures that you can re-create when you're my age. It sure takes the sting outta gettin' old," she said with a smirk.

I knew exactly what she meant. And I made a pledge to myself that day to follow in her footsteps when I reached my golden years—no matter what people thought.

A half hour after my most amazing afternoon, we were home. I went straight to my room to get a handle on my new career. I just couldn't get it out of my head. This was so amazing—all the stuff about Gram and Eugene. And now I was about to be a part of it all. I kept thinking about tomorrow—the first day of my apprenticeship. It promised to be legendary.

Later that night, I was watching TV in the living room. Mom was reading a magazine, while Dad wrestled with a newspaper on the couch. My dad was a noisy reader. When he found an interesting story, he'd fold the paper into a neat rectangle so just that article was visible. When he finished, he'd unfold it and do it all over again, a zillion times.

"Doris," my dad said, "did you see this story? The police found a body on a Miami beach. He had a fractured skull and a bunch of broken bones."

"Oooh, how terrible," she said. My mother was not a fan of gruesome details.

"But get this—the cause of death was hypothermia."

"Hypothermia? You mean he froze to death?" she said. "In Miami?"

"You think *that's* strange?! There were no footprints or tire tracks in the sand around the body." My dad set the paper on the coffee table. "So how the heck did he get there?"

As was my nature, I was conveniently listening in on my parents' conversation. It had paid dividends in the past. I thought about the clues my dad had rattled off— broken bones, hypothermia, no footprints.

"I can tell you how he got there," I said before my mother could respond. "I think the guy was dead before he broke any bones."

"Huh?" My dad seemed skeptical. "How do you figure?"

"There's only one way to freeze to death on a Miami beach. This guy had to have been a stowaway."

"Where do you come up with this stuff?" My dad was clearly challenging my logic.

"Dad, don't you see? He must have stowed away in

the landing gear of a jet. When it got to thirty thousand feet, he froze to death. Then near the end of the flight, the landing gear comes down, and he falls out. That's why there were no footprints." I loved watching the reaction on my parents' faces when they realized that I had nailed another one. "Good night," I said as I headed to my room. I looked back and noticed my parents just staring at each other. I was hoping that this might be the turning point. Maybe they would finally learn to appreciate my talents instead of always trying to stifle me. I wanted to believe that in the worst way but I knew it would never happen.

At school on Tuesday, the second hand on the clock was back to its old tricks. Never had a day seemed so long—and so unproductive. I had tried my best to talk to Scarlett every chance I could get—in class, between periods, at lunch, on the playground, you name it—but every attempt had been foiled. She was either talking to a teacher, or a group of friends, or taking a makeup exam, or was simply nowhere to be seen. I tried to convince myself that she wasn't avoiding me, but it sure looked that way. Maybe she was no longer interested in my help. I hoped that wasn't the case, but I guessed I wouldn't blame her if it was. Every time she had tried to talk to me, something or someone had always gotten in the way.

When the bell finally rang, I grabbed my backpack, bolted out the door, and continued to look for her. Twenty minutes later, I suspended the search. She had vanished. It was time to accept defeat. If a business relationship with Scarlett, or any other kind of relationship for that matter, wasn't in the cards, then I should at least try to appreciate the fact that Eugene was offering me the kind of opportunity that I had dreamed about for years. I made my way to the bus stop. I didn't want to be late for the first day of my apprenticeship at Eugene's. When I hopped on the bus, I looked around for Henry but then I remembered that his mom was picking him up for a dentist's appointment. Maybe it was for the best. I didn't want to have to explain to him where I was headed this afternoon.

"What's your rush, Charlie?" Milton said.

"Oh, nothing really."

Our bus driver, Milton Jarvis, was the nicest man I had ever met, and one of the most patient. No matter how disruptive the gang got, he never lost his cool. As long as everyone remained seated, we could be as loud as we liked. When you stepped up into his vehicle, you were always greeted with a smile. When you exited, Milton left you with a wink. I don't think the man ever had a bad day in his life.

The ride home, like everything else that day, dragged on. When we finally pulled up to my stop, I attempted to hop off but the bus door jammed. I decided not to wait for Milton to unstick it. I'd do it myself. I dropped my backpack and yanked at it.

"Relax, Charlie," Milton said. "I'll take care of it."

But I couldn't relax. The first day of my professional career was about to begin and I wasn't going to be sidetracked by a mechanical malfunction. The more I pulled, the less it budged.

"It won't move," I groaned. When I turned, Milton was standing over my shoulder with a why-don't-you-just-let-me-do-it look on his face. I backed off. Milton leaned in and began to monkey with one of the steel rollers at the top. A second later, the door slid open.

"Something must be pretty important, huh?" Milton said.

"Yeah, something important," I said. "Thanks, I'll see you later."

I hopped off and watched as the bus roared off. I decided to wait on the corner momentarily, just in case some nosy classmate tried to eyeball me from the back window. Couldn't let anyone get suspicious about my eagerness to return to the nest. For my trouble, I managed to catch a mouthful of exhaust.

When the bus was safely out of sight, I hustled down the block, up our driveway, in the back door, and into my room. I threw my backpack onto the bed and changed clothes. I ran back through the kitchen and stopped. A basket of fruit and a plate of doughnuts caught my eye. Well actually, it was the doughnuts that caught my eye. Let's see: There's the wise, healthy choice, and the choice I usually make. Which will it be today?

Now, mind you, I'm a fairly intelligent kid. This shouldn't have been a difficult decision. But I was going to have to pedal clear across town. I needed a quick burst of energy to motor these stocky legs. There, I had done it. I had justified the poor choice. I wasn't proud but at least I was decisive. I grabbed the glazed one, and by the time I reached the garage, the doughnut had left this earth. It was in a better place.

I wiped my hands on my pants and swung open the door. I stopped short, and was surprised—no, make that shocked—to see Henry sitting on a folding chair with his feet up on the card table.

"What are you doing here?" I said. "I thought you had a dentist appointment."

"He cancelled. He had a toothache."

I smiled.

"And it's a good thing," he said as reached over and picked up a yellow legal pad from the workbench. He tapped on it with his knuckle. "We've got a client. Don't you remember? I would have sent you a text to remind you but neither of us has cell phones, and even if we did, you'd never use yours."

I pulled the pad from his hands. "Oh, umm, look,

I can't do this today. We'll have to reschedule. I have to be somewhere. Sorry."

"Where?" Henry said.

I looked down at my feet. I wanted to tell him in the worst way but I just couldn't. It wasn't my call. Eugene had drawn up the rules.

"Look, just somewhere, okay," I said. "It's not important."

Henry looked at me suspiciously. "What's going on with you? Like you always say—what's more important than helping out your fellow man?"

I hated it when Henry lectured me. I hated it even more when he was right. I sighed. We had booked a client. I had to honor it. "Who's coming? How long will it take?" I asked. "One of your favorites," Henry said with a mischievous grin.

One of my favorites? Who could he be talking about—wait a minute—had he actually managed to persuade Scarlett to come back? After all the problems we'd been having trying to connect, was she about to walk through that door one more time? But how could it be? This was Henry. Knowing how he felt about Scarlett, I was sure he would never have booked her. Unless he felt bad about how things had turned out Saturday night? Of course, that was it. He knew I was teed off about the whole thing. And now he was trying to make up for it.

"Okay," I said. "I suppose I can fit in a needy client

before I have to take off." I was sure Eugene would understand if I was a few minutes late.

And right on cue, there was a tapping at the door. Henry scooted over to welcome in Eddie Akers, aka . . . Fast Eddie. Eddie had earned his nickname by the rate at which he spoke . . . and his love affair with the easy life. He was unfamiliar with the phrase *hard work*. If there was a fast and easy way to accomplish a task, Eddie was all over it.

"Hello, gentlemen, what can you do for me?" Eddie said.

Henry climbed to his feet, and held out his hand, palm up. "Let's see it, Eddie."

"See what?"

"You know what I'm talking about."

"Huh?"

"The cash. You still owe from last time."

"Oh." Eddie chuckled nervously. "I'm good for it. You know me."

"That's the problem, *Fast* Eddie, we *know* you."

Henry was not about to let Eddie pull a patented *fast* one.

"If you're looking for a little advice from Charlie here, it's gonna cost you at least a couple of bucks . . . upfront."

Eddie dug his hands into both pockets, turning them inside out. "I seem to be a little short."

"No, Eddie, *I'm* a little short . . . and you're out of luck," Henry informed the soon-to-be-ex client.

Without waiting for a response from our guest, Henry began shoving Eddie out the door, while I watched with one eye. Good, this wouldn't take long.

"Wait a minute, guys, there's something in it for you this time," Eddie pleaded.

Henry wasn't buying it. He dragged Eddie to the exit.

"Charlie, do something," Eddie said. He seemed desperate.

"Wait, Henry," I said. "Okay, Eddie, spill it."

Without waiting for an invitation, Eddie pulled up a chair and plopped down.

"Okay, here's the deal. Tomorrow at noon, there's gonna be this contest at Eli's Electronics Emporium. They're giving away a fifty-dollar gift certificate. It's sweet, let me tell you." Eddie still had not come up for air.

"What kind of contest?" I asked.

"That's the best part. It's a brainteaser." He leaned forward and grinned. "And I just happen to have an advance copy of the question."

"How'd you manage that?" Henry said.

Eddie sat back in his chair. "Let's just say I've got the inside scoop. But my contact couldn't get a copy of the answer. That's where you come in, Charlie."

"Oh, really?" I was less than thrilled at the thought of becoming an accomplice of Fast Eddie's.

"Yeah. You help me solve this brain buster and I'll give you ten percent of the winnings. Then I'll be more than paid up. What do you say?"

"Ten percent?" Henry said. "That's an insult. Let me show you to the door, Mr. Akers." Henry grabbed Eddie by the elbow and lifted him from the chair.

"Wait, wait, wait! I'm a reasonable guy. What'll it take?"

I looked at my partner. Henry handled all negotiations.

"Fifty percent or no deal," Henry said.

"Awwww!" Eddie whined. "Listen, I'm the one takin' all the risks."

"And Charlie could walk into that store at noon tomorrow and win the fifty bucks legitimately," Henry fired back. "As a matter of fact, I think that's what we'll do."

"Okay, okay. Fifty percent it is," Eddie said as he pulled a paper from his pocket and unfolded it. "Are ya ready?"

I looked at my watch. I needed to make this quick. "Fire away," I said. "And hurry up."

Henry shook his head, grabbed a handful of darts, and began tossing.

"Okay, here goes," Eddie said.

Henry stopped in mid-toss. "For Pete's sake, what is it?"

"Okay, okay. Here you go: When does the number fourteen fall between nine and eleven?"

I rested my elbows on the table in thought. I had never heard this one before. As the minutes passed, I began to panic. I couldn't believe I was stumped. I was expecting to hit a home run and run out the door. This was downright embarrassing. I scribbled some numbers on a piece of scratch paper. Nothing.

"C'mon, Charlie, think," Eddie said.

"Hey, don't pressure him," Henry warned. His last dart barely missed the bull's-eye. "Ooh."

I sighed. I was a beaten man. "Eddie, I'm sorry. I just don't know."

"You're kidding, right?" Henry said. He apparently had never heard me utter those words before.

"No, I mean it. "I can't figure it out." I glanced over my shoulder at Henry. "What do *you* think?"

He froze. First, he saw me fail to produce an answer. Then, he was asked for advice. He rolled a dart between his forefinger and thumb and thought hard. He stared a hole through the dartboard. His face reddened. Then I noticed a sparkle in his eye.

"Look," Henry shouted, pointing at the dartboard. The number fourteen was between the numbers nine and eleven.

"English darts, of course." I jumped from my chair and high-fived my friend.

"Thanks, boys," Eddie said as the door slammed behind him. His mission accomplished, Fast Eddie was gone . . . with the correct answer . . . and a step closer to a crisp new Ulysses S. Grant. I doubted I'd ever see that twenty-five dollars.

Henry folded his arms and flashed one of those I-told-you-so smiles.

"I know, I know," I said, as I folded up the card table. "Sorry, but I gotta get going."

"*Now* are you gonna tell me where you're going?"

I didn't know what to say. Henry could always tell when I was hiding something. He stood there with his head cocked to one side. He knew I'd eventually cave in. We both knew it. Oh, what the heck. After that last brain buster, maybe I should have more respect for Henry's reasoning skills. *He* solved it, not me. Plus, he was my best friend. We were partners . . . in here . . . and everywhere else. I'm sure Eugene would understand. Although just to be safe, I wouldn't tell Eugene that I had betrayed his confidence. Ooh, that sounded bad. I wouldn't tell him that I had accidentally spilled the beans. Yeah, that was better.

"All right, I'll tell you, but you can't tell another soul." I wasn't quite sure how to explain it. "So you know Eugene? From the library? He's got an office on the other side of town."

"What kind of office?"

I should have told him to sit down. This was gonna be a blockbuster. "Well, it's kind of like this place . . . but the real thing."

"He's got an office in a garage?"

He wasn't making this easy. "No, he runs his own private detective agency."

Henry looked at me, then burst out laughing.

"I'm serious. Eugene is a professional private investigator. He's been doing it for years. He worked for Naval Intelligence during the war, and after that he joined the CIA."

Henry grinned. "Okay, Charlie, if you don't want to tell me where you're going, that's fine. But don't treat me like an idiot. I'd rather you say nothing than lie to me."

"Henry, it's the truth. I swear it."

"Are you meeting a girl? Please don't tell me it's Scarlett Alexander."

"It's not Scarlett. I told you, it's Eugene."

"Just go. I'll see you tomorrow." Henry rolled his eyes and left.

What had just happened? What did I do wrong? I broke my promise not to tell anyone. And then my best friend turned on me. This wasn't fair at all. I told the truth. Bad things aren't supposed to happen when you tell the truth. The same thing happened to Sam Solomon in Episode #5—*The Dues and Don'ts Caper.* Sam had been hired by a well-known East Coast company to investigate a union steward who was suspected of siphoning funds from the membership's retirement account. When Sam informed his client that an executive VP, and not the union official, was the corrupt party, no one would believe him. The police were finally called in, but not before thousands of dollars had disappeared. I couldn't let the same thing happen. Even though it seemed unbelievable, I would somehow have to convince Henry that Eugene, the nice old man, the library volunteer, was actually a former government operative. This wouldn't be easy. I knew the whole story . . . and I was still having a hard time believing it.

CHAPTER 7

The Never on a Sundae Caper

I hopped on my bike and began my trek over to Eugene's. A few minutes into the journey, I couldn't help but notice something strange. There were flyers all over the neighborhood—plastered on every mailbox, streetlight, park bench, trash can, store window . . . you name it. I stopped to read one. It was offering a reward for a lost cockatiel. A minute later, I came across another one—asking for help in finding a lost macaw. And a few feet away, still another flyer had a picture of a missing Amazon parrot.

I thought back to Mrs. Jansen's comment in class about missing birds, and the story on the news. And yesterday at school, Scarlett started to tell me about her grandpa's missing parrot. She must have had second thoughts about asking a kid to help solve a real case, though, because I hadn't heard from her since. I couldn't say I blamed her.

I started to pedal even faster. Reading the flyers had slowed me down. When I spotted the old City Hall building, I knew I was about halfway there. I jumped off my bike and sat on the curb for a minute. I could tell I was burning calories. I couldn't ever remember breathing that hard before. My mom would love this. I should tell her about all the exercise I'd be getting from now on. Wait a minute. On second thought, maybe not. Not only was I not supposed to tell her about any of this, but my gut told me she'd never approve. Best to say nothing, and just let her notice my soon-to-be slim physique.

About fifteen minutes later, I spotted the army surplus store . . . and more missing-bird flyers. I was almost there. Just a few more blocks. I pedaled and panted and pedaled and panted. Then in the distance I could see Kendall Avenue, and seconds later, the barber shop. I had done it. As Grandma had instructed, I made sure that no one had seen me and proceeded to the back entrance. There was no place to lock my bike. I hoped the neighborhood was safe. I pulled open the stubborn back door and climbed the stairway. When I reached the entrance to Eugene's office, I was just about to knock when I remembered the code—I knocked twice, scraped my fingernails on the door and knocked three more times.

"Come in," Eugene's voice was faint.

I slowly pushed open the door.

"Well, don't just stand there. Let's get to work," Eugene said as I stepped into the office.

I closed the door, shuffled up to the desk, and sat down. "Reporting for duty, sir." I decided on a military greeting. More official.

Eugene leaned over and smiled. "It's good to see you. I'm glad you decided to take me up on my offer."

"I appreciate the opportunity."

"You're quite welcome. And you didn't tell anyone about all this, did you?"

I knew that Eugene deserved an honest response, but since Henry was a disbeliever, I figured I'd tell him what he wanted to hear.

"Not a soul."

Eugene sat back in his chair and pulled a half-eaten candy bar from his pocket. He bit off a piece, then stopped in mid-chew. "Your grandma's not out there, is she?"

"No. I came alone."

He grinned and continued his meal. "Okay, so, you ready for a little test?"

"A test?"

"Of course. I need to make sure you're worthy. Although I'm really not worried. Here we go. The first thing I'd like you to do is open the safe. You see, occasionally, we'll need a little getting-around money, and you'd better know where it's kept."

"What safe exactly are you talking about?"

Eugene shook his head. He seemed disappointed. "And you call yourself a fan?" He sighed, reached for a magazine on the desk, and began flipping pages. "Let me know when you find it."

Okay now. This was no time to panic. For some reason, he was under the impression that I would know how to find this safe. But why would he think that? I looked around. Wait a minute! I remembered that this place was a replica of Sam Solomon's office. I ran to the far wall and lifted the portrait of FDR from its hook. I smiled and waited for his approval.

"Okay, now open it," Eugene said.

I was afraid he'd say that. I set the picture on the file cabinet, and reached for the tumbler. I spun it around. Then a second time. And a third time. I was stalling. What was that combination? This was all so frustrating. I knew it. Heck, I'd quizzed people on it. *Think, Charlie.*

I turned the tumbler to 25, no 26. I was sure it was 26. Then I spun it back to . . . 9? Yeah, 9. Then onto . . . what? Of course, 37. I turned the handle, and the safe door swung open. I let out a long sigh.

"Nicely done. But next time, pick up the pace."

Our attention was suddenly drawn to the sound of footsteps in the hallway. They were soon followed by a soft knock.

Eugene pointed to the safe and whispered. "Close it up."

I locked it and slid the FDR portrait back into place.

"Now get the door," Eugene said. "Looks like we got ourselves a client."

I was afraid my heart would pound right through my chest. I marched to the door and flung it open. There was no one there. I knew I had heard someone knock. I poked my head into the hallway.

Standing a few feet away, apparently second-guessing her decision, was Scarlett Alexander.

"Charlie Collier?" she said.

I wasn't quite sure how to answer. I had never expected to see her here. Before I could muster up a greeting, she turned and began walking down the stairs.

"Scarlett . . . wait . . . don't leave." I wasn't about to let her get away. What was she doing here anyway? Unless . . . unless she was looking for me. Of course. She had followed me all the way here just to ask me to take on her case. That had to be it.

"Can I help you in any way?" I asked.

"I . . . I was looking for someone," she said.

"You found him," I said proudly.

"I was actually looking for someone else," she said.

I thought to myself for a minute. If she hadn't come here to see me, then she must be looking for . . .

"You mean Eugene?" I said.

"Yes. My grandfather sent me up here to see him."

"He's right in here. Come on in." I ran back into the office.

"Well?" Eugene said.

"There's a Scarlett Alexander here to see you."

"Does she have an appointment? We're kinda busy."

I looked around the room. Who was he kidding? I decided I had better just play along.

"I'll check." I scooted back into the hallway. "Do you have an appointment?"

"No. I just thought . . . you know, I think this is a mistake. Thanks anyway."

"No, no, no. Please come in." I glanced at my watch. "We just happen to have an opening."

Scarlett reluctantly followed me into the office. I pulled out a chair for her opposite Eugene, who stood to greet her. Then I grabbed a pad and pencil and sat down.

"Eugene Patterson, P.I. Glad to meet you, Miss Alexander, is it?"

"Yes."

Eugene nodded in my direction. "This is my new associate, Mr. Collier."

I was an associate. A real associate. I liked the sound of it. So did Scarlett. I could tell she was impressed. There was no doubt about it.

"So what brings you here?" Eugene said.

"Well, my grandpa told me you might be able to help us. I think you know him," she said. "Conor Dolan?"

"You're Conor's granddaughter? Well, how do you like that." Eugene nodded in my direction. "Conor's my landlord. He's the barber downstairs. We gotta take real good care of this little lady."

I was in complete agreement. Whatever she needed, I was on it.

"So, Scarlett, how can I help?" Eugene said.

"Well, do you know the parrot downstairs in my grandpa's shop? Socrates? He's missing. We can't find him anywhere."

"Hold on," I said. "This is the same parrot you told me about a few days ago?"

Scarlett nodded.

"Wait a minute," Eugene interrupted. He turned to me. "Do you two know each other?"

"Scarlett and I go to the same school. We're in class together."

"How do you like that?" Eugene smiled. "Small world." He sat back, folded his arms, and motioned for Scarlett to continue.

"Well, my grandpa assumed that Socrates had some-how escaped, and that we'd probably never see him again. But I just couldn't accept that. We looked and looked—everywhere." She sighed. "Then I figured we might be able to hire someone who did this sort of thing—you know, someone who finds missing people and pets and stuff—and might be able to help us locate him. And I thought I knew just the right person who could help us . . ." She glanced in my direction.

Right at that moment, I wanted to crawl into a hole.

She had come to me in need, and I wasn't there for her. I had really botched this up. I had to fix it.

"But when that didn't work out, my grandpa suggested I come up here and ask you if you might be able to help out."

Eugene scratched his head. "Sweetie, I'd sure like to help you. But we don't do lost pets." He held up his hands. "Now don't get me wrong—I'm sure old Socrates is real special to you and your grandpa, but it's just not one of the services we offer. I'm sorry."

I couldn't believe what I was hearing. Sure, one missing bird might not be a big deal, but if this was somehow related to all the other missing birds in the neighborhood, then this had all the makings of a monster case—and it just might be the big score I had been waiting for. I couldn't sit here and let Eugene turn her away. She was hurting. She was in need. And for Pete's sake, it was Scarlett.

"Please, Mr. Patterson. You don't know how important that bird is to my grandfather. They've gotten very attached over the years."

"I can appreciate that but . . ."

"Why just the other day he told me that on slow days, when the shop's empty, if it wasn't for Socrates, he wouldn't know what to do with himself." Scarlett paused. She cocked her head slightly and smiled. "They keep each other company. They have conversations like regular people. Please help us find him."

"Listen, honey, your grandpa is a good friend, and you couldn't ask for a better landlord, but I wouldn't know where to begin. If Socrates somehow got out there"—Eugene pointed to the window—"it's doubtful you'll ever see him again." He sat down and put his hands together. "Why don't you just put up some posters in the neighborhood with the parrot's picture on it—see if anyone may have spotted him?"

"I just got done doing that," she said.

"Then you've done everything you can until he shows up . . . *if* he shows up."

Scarlett sighed. She finally seemed to accept the fact that she was not about to become Eugene's next client. She dropped her head, rose from the chair, and turned to leave. "Thanks anyway," she said.

Eugene put his finger to his lips. "Now wait a minute. Maybe there is a way for you to get some help. Perhaps there's someone else who might be of assistance."

"Really? Can you recommend someone?" she said.

What was Eugene doing? He couldn't send her away.

"I know of someone who'd be perfect for this job," he said. "He's kind of young, and he hasn't been in the business very long, but I've heard some great things about him. I'll bet he just might agree to help you."

I had to do something. I couldn't lose this case. I couldn't lose Scarlett.

"I'll take the case, Eugene," I said. "I'll help her find Socrates. She doesn't have to go anywhere else."

Eugene sat back in his chair and started to chuckle.

Well, I certainly hadn't expected that reaction. I couldn't believe he was laughing at me. Didn't he think I could handle it? If he'd just give me a chance, I could show him.

"I can do it, Eugene. I know I can."

Eugene sat up in his chair. "I know you can too, Charlie. Don't you get it? *You* were the private eye I was talking about. This'll be good for you. Give you a chance to get your feet wet. Then with a little more experience under your belt, you'll be all ready to tackle the really big cases."

I walked over and shook Eugene's hand. "You won't be sorry," I said.

"I know that," he said. "Here's the deal—this is your case. You call the shots. I won't step on your toes. But I want you to keep me in the loop. If you get in over your head, don't feel like you're on your own. Come and talk to me. That's what associates do. Got it?"

"Got it," I said. "So when can I get started?"

"It's your case," he said. "It's your agenda."

I glanced in Scarlett's direction. "What are you doing right now?"

"Nothing," she said.

Eugene turned to Scarlett. "Do you mind waiting downstairs in your grandpa's shop? I'd like to talk to Charlie for a couple of minutes."

"Sure," she said. She walked to the door and stopped.

"I really appreciate this, Mr. Patterson. Grandpa is going to be so happy."

I made a beeline to the door and held it open for her.

"Glad to be of assistance," Eugene said.

"I'll meet you there in a few minutes," I told Scarlett.

She smiled and waved.

I watched her glide down the hallway. I closed the door and leaned against it. This was gonna be great. Eugene waved me over. I pulled up a chair opposite him.

"I couldn't help but sense a little chemistry in here a moment ago," he said.

"What do you mean?"

"I saw the way you looked at her."

I didn't know how to respond.

"This isn't just any girl, is it?" Eugene said. "This is *the* girl. Am I right?"

Had I been that obvious? I was a little embarrassed. For an old-timer, Eugene was pretty sharp. He had seen right through me.

"Well . . ." I couldn't quite get the words out.

"It's okay," he said. "There's nothing wrong with that. But sometimes it can get in the way—in our business especially. Remember the first commandment that every private investigator needs to obey: *Don't ever allow yourself to get personally involved with a client.* It can be dangerous."

I knew he was right. Countless times Sam Solomon

had made the same mistake. He had gotten too close to a client. And each time he vowed never to let it happen again. But Eugene had nothing to worry about. I was confident I wouldn't allow myself to fall into that trap.

Eugene leaned forward. "You always have to think with your head, and not your heart. If you forget that rule, you could lose that head of yours. Heck, you could lose your life."

"I won't forget," I said.

Eugene smiled. "Okay, you have a client waiting. Get out of here."

As I ran downstairs to meet up with Scarlett, I thought about what Eugene had said. Lose your head? Lose your life? What was he talking about? Just how dangerous could a case like this be anyway? Missing birds? C'mon. Sam Solomon would barely have worked up a sweat with a case like this. In fact, in Episode #10— *The Never on a Sundae Caper*—Sam analyzed evidence and managed to crack a smuggling case while sitting in an ice cream parlor devouring a hot fudge sundae. A good private detective can think on his feet. If I wasn't able to wrap up this thing in a day or two, then I was losing my touch. I could handle this case in no time, and I had no intentions of allowing my personal feelings to cloud my judgment. I'd earn my stripes in record time, and be ready to tackle even more challenging capers. Eugene would see. At least, I hoped so.

CHAPTER 8

The Chic Sheik Caper

Minutes later, I entered the barber shop through the back door. Conor Dolan, the owner, who was trimming a customer's beard at the time, stopped and scowled at me. "Hey, you can't come in through there."

"Grandpa," Scarlett said, "this is Charlie Collier. He works with Mr. Patterson. He's here to help us."

"Oh, sorry, son. Well, in that case, you're more than welcome. So, old Eugene's taking on a partner, huh?"

"Associate," I said.

"Oh, an associate. I see," Mr. Dolan said with a smirk.

I turned to Scarlett. "Is there anywhere we can talk . . . privately?"

"You kids can use the back room," Mr. Dolan said.

I followed Scarlett past a second barber chair and a rack of magazines, and into a small, dimly lit room.

She motioned for me to take a seat. Instead of chairs, there were a couple of stools.

"Thanks for taking on this case," she said. "To tell you the truth, when you opened that door, I was surprised to see you."

"Actually, today's my first day on the job."

"Well, I'm glad you were there." She smiled.

Me too. "So, tell me about the missing bird," I said, getting back to business.

"There's not much more to tell. A few days ago when Grandpa opened the shop, he noticed that the cage was empty. Socrates was gone. He looked everywhere. He called my mom to tell her. And then after school that day, she drove me over here. I helped look for him. One thing's for sure, Socrates isn't here. If he was, he'd tell us." She smiled. "He's a pretty good talker. He can even say my name."

"What kind of a parrot is he?" I said. "What does he look like?"

"Don't go anywhere," she said. Scarlett hopped off the stool and walked into the main barber shop area. A moment later she returned holding a photograph. She began to peel tape off the back of it. "Grandpa had this hanging on his big mirror out there." She handed it to me.

I examined the photograph. It was a picture of a green bird sitting on her grandpa's shoulder.

"He's an African yellow-faced parrot. He's mostly green, as you can see, but like the name says, his face and head are yellow. He's just beautiful."

I set the photo down on a small table. "Has he ever gotten out of his cage before?" I asked.

"He's tried. He's pretty smart. But Grandpa keeps the cage door wired shut so Socrates can't get it open."

I slid off the stool and poked my head into the shop. I just wanted to see the cage that Scarlett was referring to.

"That's it, huh?" I said.

She nodded.

"And your grandpa's sure that the wire was on the cage door the night before Socrates went missing?"

"We talked about it," she said. "He's positive."

I glanced at the cage one more time, and thought to myself for a minute.

"I don't want to jump to conclusions," I said. "But if everything you've told me is true, we've got ourselves a kidnapping . . . or rather, a birdnapping."

Scarlett seemed slightly uncomfortable. "But who . . . who would do something like that? And why?"

"That's what you're paying me to find out."

"Oh, what will all of this cost? I assume it's more than what you usually charge."

I hadn't even thought about it. I had no idea what Eugene charged his clients . . . or if he ever cut a deal for a friend.

"Let's not worry about that right now. I'll talk to Eugene. I'm sure he'll come up with a reasonable fee, considering it's for your grandpa and all."

Scarlett smiled. "Thanks."

I felt myself starting to run out of questions. I wanted to keep this conversation going on as long as possible. How many more times would I have an opportunity like this? To be alone with Scarlett with no competition around. But I also knew that it was about time to get down to business—to do some real detective work.

"One more thing," I said. "Did you check for any signs of forced entry?"

"Well, I do remember Grandpa saying that when he came in that morning, he found both the front and back doors locked."

I slid off the stool. "Do you mind if I take a look for myself?"

Scarlett led me through the shop to the front entrance. I examined the door inside and out. It was clean. No scratches. The wood frame around the door showed no signs of tampering. If we were indeed looking for an intruder, he was certainly a pro. That was for sure.

"Let's look at the back door," I said.

We made our way back through the shop, and as we passed by the barber chair, Mr. Dolan leaned over. "You sure you're up to the challenge, son? Socrates was my best friend. I just gotta get him back."

"I'll do my best, sir."

Mr. Dolan patted me on the back. Scarlett and I entered the storage room and stopped when we reached the back door. I dropped to my knees for a thorough inspection of both the doorknob and lock.

"He's good. Really good," I said.

"Who?" Scarlett asked.

"Our birdnapper," I said.

"Well, if somebody did take him," Scarlett said, "he was in for the fight of his life."

I stood up and brushed off my knees. "What do you mean?"

"Socrates doesn't like strangers. If someone had come into Grandpa's shop and tried to take him from his cage, he would have scratched and clawed and pecked them. Old Socrates was a fighter." Scarlett caught herself momentarily. "Did you hear what I just said?! I said he *was* a fighter. You've got me thinking I'll never see him again." She dropped her head.

Scarlett was beginning to lose hope. I needed her to remain optimistic and to focus on helping me track down the alleged bird snatcher.

"Did I hear you say you put up flyers in the neighborhood?" I asked.

"Yep, all over. But I don't see what good they'll do. There's dozens of them all over the area for other birds who've disappeared."

"I know. I saw a bunch of them coming over here. There's gotta be dozens of missing birds," I said. This case was becoming more and more interesting. It wasn't shaping up as a typical lost-pet dilemma. There seemed to be much more to it. And the fact that the story had made the news lately made me think that this case was getting bigger by the minute. "Do you know if any of these birds have been found?" I asked.

"Not that I know of. That's why I'm afraid we may never see Socrates again."

"Well, let's start to put some of the facts together," I said. I pulled a notepad from my back pocket. I tried to recall as many details as I could remember from the flyers. I told Scarlett that I had seen flyers for all different kinds of birds—parrots, cockatoos, cockatiels, macaws, conures, and more exotic varieties like eclectus and pionus parrots—not to mention the missing falcon and hawk that Mrs. Jansen had told us about. I explained to her that a few of the owners had indicated that some of their pet birds were wearing identification tags. And that part puzzled me. If these birds had simply gotten loose, wouldn't someone have noticed at least one of them and reported it? You don't often see exotic birds flying around loose in the Midwest. But according to Scarlett, none of the birds had been recovered.

Since the birds appeared to be all shapes and sizes and colors, it didn't take long to determine that there was no pattern here. Interestingly enough, most had disappeared from stores or shops, but a few had come people's homes. And in each case, according to the flyers, the birds had disappeared when no one was at home, or when the shops were closed. Apparently our thief had no intention of confronting an angry pet owner.

"Do you mind if I look around the back of the shop?" I said.

Scarlett led me through the back door and into the alley. I decided to perform a thorough examination of the grounds. I dropped to all fours for a better look. I crawled around for a few minutes. I must have looked pretty silly. I assumed that the thief had to have entered from the back since the front of the shop was on a busy street.

I searched until my knees ached. Then I noticed a crumpled piece of paper under a row of bushes. I grabbed it, opened it, and showed it to Scarlett. There were a bunch of letters and numbers written on it in random order, but they made no sense. The writing appeared to be red crayon.

"What'd you find?" Scarlett asked.

"I'm not quite sure." I handed the paper to her.

"It's just a bunch of scribbling," she said. "It doesn't make any sense. You might as well throw it away."

"Not so fast. A good P.I. considers every shred of evidence no matter how insignificant. Why, in Episode #6 of Sam Solomon's *The Chic Sheik Caper*, a single blade of grass bent in the wrong direction was all Sam needed to solve an international mystery. When you're dealing with the criminal element, you can't overlook a thing. What if this piece of paper belonged to the birdnapper? It might just lead us to his whereabouts."

Scarlett shook her head. "Sounds like a stretch to me."

"You may be right. It could be meaningless, but at this point in the investigation, I'm dismissing nothing."

Scarlett took another look at the paper. "Let's just say you're right. Let's say this does have something to do with the missing birds. Look at this note. It looks like it's written in crayon. Do you think that kids might be behind this?"

"It's possible. Anything's possible at this point."

"So, what do we do now?" she asked.

I wasn't really sure what to do next but I didn't want to admit that. I wanted Scarlett to have faith in me. I wanted her to think that her money was being invested wisely. I thought about what I had learned in the last half hour. And then instead of blurting out the wrong thing just to say something, I decided to take a step backward. I thought it might be a good idea to share my findings with Eugene. Although he told me that this was my case, he did say that I could bounce things off him if I needed to. I just wanted to make sure I was on the right track. I was hoping this would be the first and last time I'd need to bother him.

"I think we should go see Eugene—bring him up

to speed on all of this. We can lay out our facts for him: Number one—the bird is missing and the cage door was locked when your grandfather found it; number two—there were no signs of forced entry at either the front or back doors; and number three—it's consistent with a rash of missing birds in the area."

"I didn't think Eugene handled lost pets," Scarlett said.

"But this isn't merely a lost-bird case. It's a bona fide kidnapping. And once he sees the evidence we've collected, he'll be glad we consulted him."

Scarlett followed me back upstairs. Eugene was getting ready to close up shop for the day.

"Back so soon?" Eugene said. "Don't tell me you found Socrates already?"

"No, I'm afraid not," I said. "I just wanted to share some of our findings with you . . . if you've got a minute."

"If you need to leave," Scarlett said, "we can do this another time."

Eugene motioned for us to sit down on a couple of chairs opposite his desk. "So whatcha got?"

"Eugene, this isn't simply a lost-bird case. It's a full-blown kidnapping."

"And what makes you think that?" he said.

I explained the rationale—missing bird, closed cage door, and no signs of forced entry.

"But you still have no evidence tying these clues to a kidnapper," he said.

I pulled the piece of paper from my pocket and handed it to him. "Look at this. It may have been written by the perp."

"The *perp?*" Eugene grinned.

"The perpetrator," I said.

Eugene laughed. "I know what it stands for, Charlie. I just wondered how you made that assumption."

"Well, you see, we found that note a few yards away from where the bird was last seen. So it might have been written by the kidnapper."

He read the note. "And this is your proof? It's jibberish. It doesn't say anything."

"I know, but—"

"Listen, kids, while you were gone, I called an old friend over at the police station. I asked him about this missing-birds business."

I always knew it paid to have contacts at the department. "So, what'd he say?" I asked.

"Their theory is that either a bunch of teenagers are out there pulling pranks, or some overzealous animal rights activist is trying to free all the caged-up critters. Take your pick. But my money's on the kids. Either way, don't expect much from the police—at least not right away. This whole thing is not what you'd call *a high priority item* for them."

"So why do you think it was teenagers, Eugene?" I asked. "Did he say there were any witnesses?"

"One of the shopkeepers apparently saw a tall, hefty

kid running from his property the other night. A few minutes later the owner noticed his cockatiel was missing." Eugene raised his eyebrows. "Looks like kids to me." Eugene took a second look at the note. "And if that isn't good enough for you, look at the writing on this paper of yours. That's crayon. Trust me, this is a just bunch of mischievous kids with nothing to do."

"So, what do you suggest we do?" I said.

"You gotta keep digging. A good P.I. weighs all the facts. And it seems to me that there are plenty more out there."

I smiled. "Thanks, you've given me a lot to think about."

"You don't have to thank me. You're part of this agency. We share with each other." He winked. "Hey, you kids better get a move on. Your parents'll be expecting you for dinner soon."

"Thank you, Mr. Patterson," Scarlett said.

"Good luck, you two," Eugene said as we slipped out into the hallway.

As we walked back to the barber shop, I knew that things rested solely on my shoulders. Eugene seemed to believe that this was just a prank. And he just might be right. I would need a whole lot more evidence to prove my point. And I wasn't sure if I could handle this thing alone. What I needed right now was an assistant—in the worst way. I was enjoying the time with Scarlett but she was no shamus . . . and it wouldn't be right asking the client to do legwork.

I knew what I had to do. I had to convince Henry that this whole Eugene thing was legitimate. I'd offer to bring him to the office after hours if necessary. Henry didn't have a mind like mine but he was logical. I had to bring him on board, bring him up to speed, and bring home a winner.

CHAPTER 9

The Roamin' Soldier Caper

I wasn't able to find an opportune moment to talk to Henry at school on Wednesday, so I waited for him at the bus stop that afternoon. When he arrived, it seemed as though he was avoiding me. I could tell he was still a little peeved about our conversation the day before. I felt bad but I didn't know why. I hadn't done anything wrong. I had told him the truth. Why did I somehow feel guilty? I needed to put this behind us, and quickly.

"Listen, Henry, I want to tell you what's going on, but you gotta believe me this time."

"If you're gonna tell me the same garbage about Eugene, the private detective, then save your breath. I'm not interested."

"Why can't I make you believe me?"

"Because it's ridiculous. You must think I'm stupid if you expect me to buy a lame story like that." He dropped his backpack to the ground. "All right, you want me to believe you? Let's go over to the library and I'll ask Eugene for myself."

"You can't do that."

"Figures."

"He'll never admit to it. He told me not to say anything. If he knew I told you . . ."

"Then we have nothing to talk about."

I somehow had to persuade him to join me. Maybe if I told him everything—about my grandmother, about Scarlett, about the lost birds—maybe then he'd buy in. Heck, he'd know I could never make up a story that good. When the bus pulled up, he stepped in front of me and climbed in. He sat in an outside seat and blocked my path so I couldn't sit next to him. I refused to allow this little spat to continue. I sat directly behind him, and for the next twenty minutes, I proceeded—in a whisper of course—to fill his head with details until it exploded.

"Eugene is a real private eye . . . he worked for Naval Intelligence in the war . . . my grandmother too . . . she helped him crack enemy codes for the Allies . . . after that she joined forces with Eugene at their own detective agency . . . then the other day, Scarlett strolls into the office . . ."

I never took a breath. About three-quarters of the way through the epic, he turned around. From that point on, I knew I had him.

"So, how is this gonna work then?" he said. "If you're working for Eugene, and I'm working with you, how much do we charge, and how do we split it up?"

Once the topic had changed to the collection of fees, I could tell that things were finally back to normal.

Later that afternoon Henry and I sat around in my room mulling over the case. I showed him the piece of paper with the jibberish written in crayon. I shared my theory with him about the note being written by the birdnapper, but neither of us was really sure what we were looking at. We just weren't certain how to proceed. This case had presented us with so little evidence. I kept waiting for something to miraculously pop into my head but there were no lightbulb moments. I began to wonder if my only true skill was solving brainteasers. Here I was, facing the real deal, and unable to click. I tightened all the muscles in my body. I closed my eyes and gritted my teeth. I would come up with a solution if it was the last thing I did.

"If you try any harder, you're going to hurt yourself," Henry said.

I exhaled. "Why is this one so tough?"

"Why don't we get on the Internet and search for an answer?"

"Not interested. I prefer solving cases in the purest way possible. We don't need high-tech devices. Sam

Solomon didn't need the Internet. Case in point—Episode #12—*The Roamin' Soldier Caper.* Sam tracked down a conman who impersonated a G.I., and then who tried to finagle his way onto the Fort Knox complex for a shot at the mother lode. And, oh, did I mention that Sam managed to capture his suspect without the use of a cell phone, a GPS, or the Internet?"

"Okay, but look at all the jams he got himself into," Henry said. "Just think how much more efficient he might have been with even a netbook tucked away in his trench coat pocket."

"No computers," I said. "It's gotta be brainpower or nothing."

"Why don't we at least network a little then?"

"I said no computers."

Henry plopped down on the bed. "No, I mean a network of people. Hit the pavement. Branch out. Pick some brains. It sure sounds like something Sam would do, right?"

Henry knew which buttons to push to win me over. "Okay . . . what do you have in mind?" I said.

"What about your buddy Eugene?" Henry said.

"I know he'd help us if we asked," I said. "But I'd really like to show him that I can do this on my own, that he made the right decision to bring me on board. For now, let's consider other options."

"What about your parents?"

"Are you nuts? If they got wind that we were taking on clients again, I'd be grounded for . . . for . . . I don't even want to think about it."

"All right then," Henry said. "How about somebody at school like Mrs. Jansen? She's pretty smart. Maybe she could help."

"I like the way you're thinking. But if we talk to a teacher, it'll more than likely get back to my parents. My mom volunteers at school a lot."

A noise from outside interrupted our conversation. We both ran to the window. Gripping the nozzle of a hose with both hands, Grandma was spraying water in the direction of the garage.

"Of course! Why didn't I think of it? We can ask my gram for help."

"Yeah, if she did this sort of work in the old days, she might have some ideas," Henry said.

When we reached my grandmother, she was huddled behind a pair of garbage cans, pelting the garage door with a jet of water.

"Hey, boys!" Grandma yelled out. "Get in this bunker with me."

We crouched down and scooted over. Gram was dressed in full army fatigues, complete with helmet.

"That band of brigands over there is all that stands between us and the kaiser." She stood up, gripped the water nozzle like a machine gun, and continued her assault on the unsuspecting garage door. She then ducked back down behind the garbage cans. "That'll give 'em something to think about."

"Gram, can we talk to you?"

Grandma looked over her shoulder at an imaginary comrade. "Hey, Murphy, keep me covered. I gotta conference with a couple of civilians for a minute." She crawled over to where we were sitting. "What can I do for you, fellas?"

"Well . . ." I didn't quite know where to begin.

She set down the hose and smiled. It seemed as though she had returned to the present . . . for at least that moment.

"So, how are things going"—Gram paused momentarily and glanced at Henry—"with you know who?"

I smiled sheepishly. "Henry knows, Gram. I told him everything."

She seemed to think to herself for a minute. "Well, what the heck? Henry's like a member of the family anyway. I don't suppose Eugene'll mind."

Henry grinned. To show his appreciation for her vote of confidence, he saluted Grandma. "Thanks, Mrs. Collier," he said.

Gram smiled and returned the gesture. She nodded for me to continue.

"Well, Gram, things are actually going pretty good. I'm working on a real case, and Eugene's letting me handle it myself."

"That's great," she said. She then held up a finger

for me to wait a moment. She slowly lifted her head from behind the garbage cans and seemed to carefully survey the area. Her head suddenly snapped to the right. "Murphy, keep your eyes open. It's too quiet out there." Gram ducked back down. "Continue," she said.

"But, Gram, to tell you the truth, this case has us stumped."

Henry stuck his head up and looked around. It almost seemed as if he were actually expecting to witness an invasion.

Grandma reached over and pushed him back down.

"Ahh, I've heard you say that before, Charlie. And you always seem to figure things out."

"Not this time."

Grandma unsnapped the strap on her helmet, pulled it off, and set it in her lap.

"Honey, you've got a gift. You just gotta be patient. Something'll pop into your head. It always does. Who knows . . . a minute from now, you might have it all figured out."

"Maybe you're right," I said, but I really didn't think so. I turned to leave, then hesitated. I dug into my pocket and pulled out the note that we had found behind the barber shop. "Gram?"

"Yep?"

I handed her the note. "What do you make of this? I found it a little while ago behind the barber shop. I don't know what to think."

She studied the gibberish on the note.

U-P 1-81-13-77-65-5-5 65-45-81-13-41-81

"To tell you the truth, it looks like some kind of code to me."

"A code?" Of course, it was a code. And that was Gram's specialty in the war. This was perfect. I wondered if she still had the gift. "Can you tell us what it says?"

She studied it for a minute. "It's a code for sure—a pretty simple one actually. Nothing like the ones I saw when I was helping out Uncle Sam. All this person did was substitute letters with numbers and vice versa."

"You mean like *a* would be number one, and *b* would be number two and so on?" Henry said.

"It's not that simple," she said. "Whoever wrote this note assigned letters with numbers, and the other way around, but they added a little twist." She held up the note for us to see. "There are three words here. The first word is all letters, which means it's a number. The second and third words are made up of numbers, so those would be letters."

It was so neat to watch Gram in her element. I tried to imagine her deciphering an enemy code during the war. I would have loved to have seen her in action.

"But instead of making the letter *a* represent a one, and *b* a two, like Henry said, they've changed the pattern between the first word and the next two words," Gram continued. "The letter *k* appears to be the number one for both patterns. And then, for the first word, the next letter, *l*, isn't a two, it's a four. So this person added three to every letter that followed. With the next two words, he changed the pattern to a difference of four from one letter to the next."

"My head's spinning, Mrs. Collier. How do you do it?" Henry said.

"The same way that Charlie solves brainteasers. It's a gift, I guess."

"So, what's it say, Gram?"

She seemed to be counting to herself for a few moments, then smiled. "It's an address. It says Thirty-one . . . sixteen . . . Kendall . . . Avenue. That's it. Hey, that sounds familiar. Wait a minute, that's Eugene's address."

"*And* the barber shop's," I said. It was at that moment that I knew we were on to something. This note had to be connected to the bird heist.

"Hey, that was fun," Gram said. "Got any more?"

"That's it for now," I said. "But we'll keep looking."

Grandma took a closer look at the note. She rubbed her finger across the words.

"What are you doing?" Henry said.

"There's something funny about this writing," she said.

"We're guessing it's crayon," I said.

She held the note up to her nose and smelled it. "This isn't crayon . . . it's lipstick. And not a very attractive shade, I might add. I wouldn't be caught dead in this color." She handed me the paper. "Anything else?" she said.

"That's it, I think. Thanks a lot."

"Well, I better get back to the firefight." She placed her helmet back onto her head, picked up the hose, grabbed the nozzle, and smiled. "Don't worry. You boys'll figure things out." A second later the battle had resumed. Water splashed off the garage door in all directions.

As we made our way back to my room, I was deep in thought about this case. I couldn't get it out of my head. After talking to Grandma, I felt certain that the note definitely belonged to the perp. But who was he? And where would I find him? Was I any closer to solving this case? *I* hadn't accomplished anything. Gram had figured it out. I still wasn't sure I could pull this off. One piece of evidence had surfaced—that was great—but there were still so many holes. I had no idea what the next move would be.

I thought about what Gram had said. She was certain that I would figure things out—all on my own— and it could happen any minute. I could only hope she was right. Why did she seem to have more faith in me than I did in myself? I wanted to take her advice. Just be patient, I told myself. Stop trying to force it. Maybe something would just suddenly pop into my head. I had to have confidence in myself. I just needed to—wait a second. I pulled the note from my pocket and stared at—an address—written in lipstick.

"Wait a second. What's wrong with me? Duh! If this thing's written in lipstick, we're not looking for a villain, we're looking for a *villainess*," I announced.

"Of course," Henry said, "the bad guy's a woman."

I smiled. It was another clue. A big one. I was now juiced. "We may just be able to pull this off, partner."

Suddenly I was ready for whatever challenge lay before me. I began to believe that I *could* do this. With Henry by my side, and with Scarlett's help, and with Eugene waiting in the wings, and, of course, with my ace in the hole—Grandma—there was no stopping this Snoop for Hire now.

At school on Thursday, Henry and I discussed the case every spare moment we had. I didn't want to tell Scarlett what we had discovered—not yet at least. I decided to wait until we had turned up more evidence. No need to get her hopes up since all of this was guesswork. We continued discussing the case over lunch. We were always careful never to let anyone overhear us . . . or so we thought.

"Remember, we need to concentrate on a female mastermind," I said.

"Yeah, I wish we knew her angle in all of this," Henry said.

"Hey, what are you guys talkin' about?" Sherman Doyle asked as he came up to our lunch table.

How could we have been so careless? This was the last guy we wanted to encounter, let alone include in our conversation.

"Did I hear you say something about them missing birds?" he said.

"Maybe. You know something about them?" I asked.

"Some."

"Well, then spill it," Henry said. "Some creep's been kidnapping exotic birds, and no one seems to know where they are."

"Maybe the guy's got a good reason for stealin' 'em," Sherman said. "Did you ever think about that?"

"Like what?" I said. I knew Sherman was a loser . . . but to defend such a dastardly deed . . . it seemed even beneath this big dope.

"Just maybe he knows something that you don't know," Sherman said, "and that's why he's taking 'em."

It was just about then that I noticed something strange. Sherman had cuts and scratches all over his hands.

"What happened?" I asked.

He pulled down his sleeves and tried to cover them up. "Nothing. Just got into a little fight, that's all."

"I'd hate to see the other guy," Henry said.

"Huh? Oh yeah. I tore him to shreds. Hey, can either of you guys break a fifty?" Sherman seemed to want to change the topic. He pulled a fifty-dollar bill from his pocket. "The lunch lady doesn't like big bills."

Henry stared at the cash. "Where'd you get that kind of money?"

Sherman jammed it back into his pocket. "Oh, just forget it," he said. And with that, he was off.

Henry looked at me and shook his head. "What planet is that guy from? Come on. Let's go."

But I couldn't move. Not yet. For the moment, I was deep in thought. What are the chances, I wondered?

"You comin'?" Henry said. When I failed to answer, he waved his hand in front of my face. "Hey, what's up?"

"I was just thinking."

"About what?"

"About Sherman. And those scratches on his hands."

"What about 'em?" Henry said. "You heard him. He got in a fight. That's all."

"I was thinking about something Scarlett told me earlier . . . about Socrates . . . about how he didn't like strangers . . . about how he'd chew up anybody who might have tried to kidnap him."

"So what are you saying?"

"Henry, those cuts on Sherman's hands . . . He *could* have gotten them in a fight . . . but maybe it wasn't an ordinary fight . . . maybe he was scuffling with . . . a *bird* perhaps? An unfriendly bird? Named Socrates?"

"Sherman? He's too dumb to pull something like that off."

"Maybe he's not doing it alone."

We hesitated for a moment as Scarlett and her entourage passed by. She looked really good today. She was on her cell phone—as usual. Henry snapped his fingers in my face.

"Earth to Charlie."

"Have you ever noticed—the only time she ever talks to me is when she needs something?" I said.

"And you just figured that out?"

I shrugged.

"Just let it go," Henry said. "It's time to get back to work."

I knew he was right. It made no sense to wish for something that would never happen. She was simply out of my league. I had always known that. "You're right. Okay, what were we talking about?"

"Sherman and the birds."

"Oh yeah."

"He could be telling the truth, you know, about getting into a fight," Henry said. "Sherman, if you haven't noticed, is no stranger to fisticuffs."

"Okay. But wait—there's the cash in his pocket."

"I *was* kind of wondering about that," Henry said.

"Maybe he had a birthday or something." He thought to himself for a moment. Then his eyes opened wide. "Or . . . are you thinking what I'm thinking? It's the payoff for heisting the birds."

"Precisely. And did you notice how he defended the kidnapper? Why would he even care about that unless he was somehow involved?"

"He did, didn't he?"

And suddenly I thought about another clue. "Eugene said that when Scarlett's grandpa was talking to some of the other shopkeepers, one of them said he saw a big kid coming out of one of the stores after hours one night. It all fits."

"Okay, let's say you're right. Let's say Sherman's our man. How are you gonna find out for sure? You gonna go up and ask him if he's the culprit? If that's your plan, I don't want to be around."

"He's not gonna talk, Henry. We both know that." I thought to myself for a moment. "Although I'll bet, with my advanced interrogation skills, I just might be able to break him."

Henry grinned. "Oh, really? More likely, he'll break you . . . in half."

He was right. We needed a new strategy.

"I guess we could just follow him," Henry said.

I nodded. There was nothing like resorting to good old-fashioned field surveillance. "That's the plan then. We'll tail him. Tonight."

"What should we tell our folks?"

"Why don't we say something like we got a big paper . . . a team project—due tomorrow—and we need to do research at the library."

"The library closes at nine," he said. "I guarantee our suspect makes his move later than that."

"Okay, then. You tell your folks that we're writing the paper at my house, and I'll tell mine that we'll be at your place—and it could get a little late."

The bell rang for fifth period. We nodded at each other to confirm our plans. The table was now set.

CHAPTER 10

The Buoys and Girls Caper

Maybe it was just the guilt consuming me but at dinner that night when I announced my plans to work on a homework project at Henry's, my parents seemed unusually combative.

"You have a paper due tomorrow and you're waiting until tonight to write it? How smart is that?" my dad said.

"It was the first time Henry and I could get together to work on it."

"What are you talking about?! The two of you are always together."

"We just found out our topic the other day." I should have anticipated this line of questioning. It wasn't one of my better efforts.

"Well, it's probably gonna look like a rush job. Is that what you want?"

"Dad, I'm at my best when the pressure's on. I'm a crammer. I can pull it off."

He stewed for a moment, then shook his head. I had survived the worst of it.

"I better get over to Henry's."

"You have a key?" my mom asked.

I nodded.

"Remember, your curfew is ten o'clock," my dad warned. "Don't be late, or you'll be placed under house arrest, got it?"

"I got it." I smiled and kissed my mom on the cheek. I didn't always do that but I needed to soften her up in the event I missed my deadline. She was always easier to sweet-talk than my dad.

I met up with Henry about a block from Sherman's house. We were on foot. We thought it would be a better idea than taking our bikes. Then, if Sherman suspected that he was being tailed, we could just dart behind a tree or a mailbox or something. This neighborhood seemed different from ours. Neither of us was particularly comfortable in this part of town. If you were alone, it was the last place you'd want to be. The streetlights had just gone on. We waited a few minutes before proceeding.

"This could be a complete waste of time, you know," Henry said.

"Then again it could be the key to solving this case. You have to stay positive."

A car filled with teenage boys roared by. I prayed that they wouldn't see us. No luck. As they sped past, they uttered a few well-chosen expletives just for effect. We continued on just past Sherman's house, trying to appear inconspicuous. When we were sure it was dark enough, we took refuge behind a row of evergreens. From our vantage point, we could see the front door and into the backyard—just in case our suspect made a hasty rear door exit.

We were fortunate that the bushes were rather sparse. We knelt down behind them for cover but were still able to see right through. Henry pulled out a deck of cards.

"What's your pleasure?"

"How are we supposed to play cards in the dark?"

"You brought a flashlight, right?"

"Yeah."

"Okay, so what do you wanna play?" Henry said.

"I'm not gonna waste the batteries on that. We may need them later."

Henry shuffled the deck. "I have a feeling he'll never show, and we'll have wasted the entire night."

"That's possible," I said.

"Then why are we here?" Henry was getting a little edgy.

Why couldn't he realize that in this profession, you needed to make an investment . . . sow a few seeds . . . pay some dues? That way you'd feel like you had earned it when things panned out.

"Listen," I said. "Sam Solomon was known to have spent a lot of time crouched down in the front seat of his car, perched in a tree, or stuffed into a closet, just to gain a glimpse of a blackmailer, forger, embezzler, or some other undesirable. Take, for example, Episode #7—*The Buoys and Girls Caper*. Sam hid in the hull of a houseboat on San Francisco Bay for four nights just to catch a smuggler who was recruiting teenage girls to help move a stash of knockoff cashmere sweaters." I smiled proudly. "So there."

Henry was unimpressed. "Well, if you're not interested in a game, at least hold the light over here so I can play some solitaire."

I placed the flashlight in my pocket and folded my arms. I refused to waste the light. One of us had to exercise good judgment.

When Henry finally realized that I was not about to cooperate, he went on the offensive.

"Okay, genius, when does four minus one equal five?"

"Hmmm, give me a minute."

"Take your time. We got all night," Henry said. His comment was more sarcastic than gracious. He would have liked nothing better than to have stumped me with this one . . . at this particular time. When does four minus one equal five? I knew immediately that this was not a math problem. I needed to think anything but logically. Can the number four take on a different shape or meaning? I started to press. And whenever I did, my thought process slipped into slow motion. I took a deep breath.

"Why don't I just tell you?" Henry said.

"No. Absolutely not." Even if it did take all night, I was not about to surrender. I concentrated for several minutes. Nothing was clicking. And then I thought— what's the harm? He had been waiting for this moment all his life. Let him enjoy it. It might be worth it just to see the look on Henry's face when he bested me. But just as I was about to throw up the white flag, something hit me. "Four minus one equals five . . . when we're dealing with Roman numerals. A four is I-V. Take away the one and you've got just the V, the five."

Henry grumbled. "Just turn on the stupid flashlight. I'm playing cards."

And just as I was about to cave in, about to switch on the light, I heard a voice coming from Sherman's front porch.

"Wait a minute," I whispered. "I think that might be him."

"Are you sure?"

"It's gotta be." I reached into my back pocket for a pair of portable binoculars that I had borrowed from my dad's dresser drawer. The minute I peered through them, I knew we had found our man. "It's him, all right," I said.

Sherman stepped out, slammed the door behind him, and ran down the stairs. The hunt was officially on. He appeared to be carrying some sort of sack under his arm. We began our pursuit.

We followed him for a couple of blocks, maintaining about a fifty-yard distance from our suspect at all times. He seemed to be avoiding well-lit streets, preferring alleys instead. I was never a fan of walking down a dark alley at night. I sure was glad Henry was alongside.

Every stick, stone, or tin can that crossed Sherman's path received a gargantuan boot from the man-child. The kid was a human bulldozer. Fearful that Sherman might detect us, we made it a point to duck down behind parked cars, garbage cans, anything that offered cover. If our boy knew we were on his trail, it could make for a very unpleasant experience.

We kept him in our sights for the next twenty minutes. He never looked back. When he reached a strip mall, a little over a mile from where we had started, he stopped and pulled what appeared to be a piece of paper from his pocket—the address of the next victim, no doubt. We followed him to the rear of the shops, where deliveries were made. We hid behind a minivan in the parking lot. He stopped at a door marked BIRD WORLD. He reached into his pocket again and pulled out something else. He slid it into the lock, fumbled with it for a moment, then turned the knob, and entered the store. The entry was swift and clean. Either Sherman had a key or he was a pro at jimmying a lock. The next few moments were deathly quiet . . . eerily quiet.

"I don't like it," Henry said.

"What do you suppose he's doing in there?"

"Maybe we should try to get a little closer and find out."

"I don't think that's a very good idea," I said. Henry could be a hero if he wanted to but I was fine with staying put until Sherman emerged from the shop.

"Where exactly are we? Do you have any idea?" Henry asked.

"Not really, no. I just figured we'd have to retrace our steps to make it back home."

"Now, that's a brilliant plan," Henry said sarcastically. "Did you ever hear of a GPS device? You don't think something like that might come in handy tonight?"

"Like Sam Solomon, we can use the stars as our guide," I said confidently. I really had no idea how to do that but I needed a comeback. We both glanced skyward at the same moment. It was overcast. There were no stars.

Henry smirked and rolled his eyes.

This little spat might have escalated had Sherman not reappeared. The empty sack he had carried into the pet shop was now full. Sherman threw it over his shoulder. It was hard to believe that there might be a living creature in there, although there was no movement or even a peep from the sack itself. So how was that possible unless . . . Wait a minute! Had he killed the poor thing? What kind of monster was this kid? I immediately thought of Scarlett. I couldn't bear telling her what we had seen.

Sherman soon returned to his less-traveled byways. We followed him for what seemed like hours until we reached an area with open fields on the outskirts of town. He plopped down next to a rotted-out oak tree. We were proud of the way we had tailed the big lug. He never once seemed to sense that he was being shadowed.

Minutes later, we could hear the sound of a motor, and within seconds a blue pickup truck, with its headlights off, pulled up alongside Sherman. He jumped up and waved to the driver, who stepped out and slammed the door. We ducked down behind some bushes. We couldn't really hear their conversation but we did notice the driver—a large figure with dark hair. I couldn't tell whether it was a woman or not. I pulled out the binoculars for a better look. It was a lady all right. She was tall and wide. She had to be at least six foot five and probably tipped the scales at 250 to 275. My mom was known to carry a lot of weight, but she was nowhere near the size of this gal. The mystery figure wore a dark trench coat that was stretched tightly around her. She reached into the front seat of the pickup and pulled out a lantern. When she held it up, we caught a glimpse of her face.

This was a face you'd never forget—full of deep wrinkles. Her features were rough, and she wore thick red lipstick. She slipped her hand into the front pocket of her trench coat and emerged with a wad of bills. She pointed to the sack Sherman was holding. He turned it over and emptied its contents onto the ground. Oh God! Henry grabbed my arm. Lying on the grass were three birds—big ones—and they were all motionless.

"Are they dead?" Henry whispered.

"Sure looks that way."

The driver dug back into her trench coat pocket and pulled out a piece of paper. She seemed to be telling Sherman something but we couldn't make it out. She held up the paper, and then pointed in the direction of the highway. She handed it to him, then proceeded to pick up each bird by its feet, flinging them, one by one, into the back of the pickup. She hopped into the cab and drove off. Sherman studied the note for several seconds, crumpled it up, and tossed it aside. He then headed in the direction he had come from.

"Come on," Henry said. "Let's see where he's headed."

I was deep in thought. I couldn't process his request.

"Aren't you coming?" he said.

There was no need to follow Sherman any longer. I was fairly certain his mission tonight had been accomplished.

"He may strike again," Henry said. "We have to stop him."

"Henry, we've seen enough. We now know there's an evil mastermind. And we know it's a woman. Gram was right about that note written in lipstick. We also know the location of the rendezvous, and we know there's a payoff. They won't meet up again tonight. If Sherman was going to strike again, he would already have done so. Then he would have delivered both shipments at the same time."

Henry kicked at the dirt. He seemed to know that my logic was sound, but it was never easy for him to accept it.

"So what's our next move then?" he said.

"I want to examine the ground over there where the truck was parked. Maybe we'll find a clue to help us identify the mystery woman."

I stood up and brushed the dirt from my knees. I started in the direction of the bird drop when Henry grabbed my arm.

"Why don't we just go to the police and tell them what we saw? They'll pull in Sherman and wrap up this whole thing."

"According to Eugene, the police aren't convinced that someone is kidnapping—or should I say, killing—these birds. They're treating it as a low priority. I'm afraid it's up to us to solve this one."

I knew that contacting the police might make both of us feel less nervous about this whole thing, but I also knew that it was still too early to do so. We needed to continue the investigation for a while longer.

"I can be very persuasive," Henry said. "I can make them believe us."

"We don't have any evidence. All we have is a wild story."

I tried to imagine the look on a police officer's face if we attempted to piece together our facts. We might be laughed out of the station. I had to convince Henry that more homework needed to be done.

"What are you talking about?" Henry said. "We can tell 'em we saw Sherman heist the birds from the pet shop. When the owner shows up in the morning, he'll be able to confirm that. And then they haul in Sherman for questioning and make him talk."

Henry was so naïve sometimes.

"And if Sherman denies everything, where's the proof?" I said. "There is none. It's our word against his. They'll eventually have to let him go. And then what do you suppose is gonna happen to us when Sherman discovers who ratted him out?"

Henry sighed. "Okay, you made your point."

I switched on the flashlight and we worked our way to the clearing where Sherman had handed over the merchandise. I immediately looked for tire tracks. The grass was so thick that there was no way to make out any patterns.

"What are we looking for?" Henry asked.

"I don't know exactly." I knew that we had seen a blue pickup truck. At least I was fairly certain it was blue. But I wasn't really sure what shade. "Hey, did you notice something funny about that old lady?"

"Other than the fact that she was gargantuan?"

"I mean how she was dressed. That trench coat. There was something weird about it."

"I didn't notice anything," Henry said.

"It just didn't look right, but I can't seem to put my finger on it." I tried to form a mental image of the trench coat but it wasn't helping. There was something there but I'd just have to wait for it to pop into my head at a later time. I decided to put it out of my mind and instead tried to concentrate on the immediate surroundings. I dropped to one knee for a better look. I aimed the flashlight at my feet. "Hmm, that's odd."

"What?" Henry said.

I picked up a handful of what appeared to be loose, dried yellow grass.

"What is it?" he asked.

I examined it closely.

"It's just dried grass," he said. "What's the big deal? We're in a prairie. There's a lot of grass around here."

"But look around. There's nothing else like it. All the other grass is green."

Henry grabbed the flashlight from my hand and waved it around. "You know, you're right."

"I think we've stumbled onto another clue."

"What?"

"You know what this is, don't you?" I said. "It's hay. And you know where you find hay? In a barn. And that means a farm, no doubt."

"Come to think of it," Henry said, "I'm pretty sure there's a farm or two around here. I know my mom's come out this way to buy fruit at a farmers' market."

I smiled. "We're slowly but surely compiling evidence." I took the flashlight back from Henry. "Maybe there's something else out here that might help." We continued to walk in circles—concentric circles—each one bigger than the last. We were determined to find anything that might lead us to Mr., or rather, Mrs. Big.

"What's that over there?" Henry said.

I aimed the flashlight in the direction he was pointing. There was a piece of paper, crumpled up, on the ground. I retrieved it, opened it, and held it out for both of us to see.

"Another note . . . in code," Henry said.

Like the last one, this note also appeared to be written in lipstick. And like before, there was a series of nonsensical letters and numbers on it.

"This has to be the paper that the old lady gave Sherman," I said. "It must be the address of the next heist."

"We gotta show this to your grandma," Henry said.

"We *could* do that, I suppose."

"What do you mean? Why wouldn't we?"

"Wouldn't you love to try to decode this thing ourselves? You heard my grandma explain how she did it. We could do the same thing. Then *we'd* be cryptologists."

"I suppose we could take a stab at it," Henry said. "But something tells me we're gonna end up needing her."

"Maybe . . . and maybe not. You gotta have faith, partner."

Henry shrugged his shoulders. He obviously didn't have faith in our abilities to solve this riddle.

"C'mon, let's get out of here," I said. "We've got a code to break. The fate of the free world may depend on it."

Henry rolled his eyes.

"Well, maybe not. It just sounded good."

The Common Scents Caper

To a kid, Friday has got to be the best day of the week. And if that Friday happens to be the last day of school before spring break, then it's even better. It was hard to concentrate in class that day but Henry and I forced ourselves to. Between periods, we would attempt to crack the code from the note we had found the night before. Repeated efforts had proven unsuccessful, but I was confident that in time we would solve it. Henry was lobbying me to bring in my grandmother. I knew that I might eventually have to but not before we had exhausted every possible solution. I really wanted to prove to both Grandma and Eugene that I was capable of solving a case on my own. But I wouldn't let pride get in the way either. If I got really stuck, I was prepared to seek out their help. It wouldn't be fair to the client not to take advantage of every available resource.

Every so often I would have to remind myself

that even Sam Solomon would occasionally call in a marker—an expert who could provide specialized information that might be difficult for Sam to uncover on his own. Like in Episode #2—*The Common Scents Caper*—Sam had been hired by a distraught wife whose husband had recently been acting in a peculiar manner. It didn't take Sam long to discover that the man's altered personality had occurred shortly after he had started using a new aftershave. The veteran detective called upon the services of an old friend, a retired chemistry professor, to help analyze the scent. The results showed traces of a rare mind-control drug. Apparently this particular manufacturer wanted to create not only a legion of loyal customers, but also a fresh-smelling army prepared to follow his every command. Soooo . . . if Sam could seek out experts in the field, I could do so as well—when and if that might be necessary, of course.

Henry and I continued decoding for most of the day, but we also found time to rehash other findings from our stakeout the night before. Neither of us was prepared to approach Sherman about his role in this mystery, nor did we want to share the grim news with Scarlett. As the day went on, it was becoming increasingly difficult to pay attention in class. My mind kept wandering. I was trying to imagine who this large, ugly, old woman might be, and why she was paying Sherman for these birds. I knew that we eventually needed to tell Scarlett what we had seen last night. It wasn't going to be easy. I didn't want to think about her reaction. But I had to come clean.

When the bell finally rang, Henry and I gathered up our stuff and scooted to the bus stop. I knew I'd delayed long enough. I had to drop the bomb—tell Scarlett that her grandfather's bird was probably dead. I would share my findings with her at the barber shop after school. She'd be expecting an update on the case.

"All ready for the ride over to Eugene's? I gotta break the news to him that you've joined the team."

"Today? Oh no. My mom rescheduled that dentist appointment. Maybe you can tell him about me tomorrow. What do you think?"

"Yeah, okay. I just gotta pick a good time and break it to him gently. We'll figure it out."

The bus pulled up and we hopped on.

An hour or so later, on the bike ride across town, I had a lot of time to think about how I'd break the news to Scarlett. It wasn't going to be easy. I was hoping she would handle it calmly. She didn't seem like the kind of girl who would just start bawling. I would tell her that it wasn't a certainty that Socrates was dead. I just didn't want her to get her hopes up that we would definitely find him alive.

I made it to the shop a few minutes early. Eugene was in the chair getting his hair cut and munching on a candy bar.

"Well, if it isn't my long-lost associate," Eugene said with a grin. "Listen, Charlie, I got a call this morning—from a prospective client—a fellow who thinks his partner may be embezzling funds from their company. I told him I wasn't sure I had the manpower right at the moment to handle the case. How close are you to wrapping up this missing-bird caper? I could use your help with this."

I wasn't sure how I should answer. I knew that the sooner I solved this case the better it would be for all of us. We were close, and getting closer every day. But I didn't want to rush things and get sloppy. It was best to fess up.

"Eugene, I still think I need a couple more days to put a lid on this one. But as soon as I'm done, I'll be right back by your side. I promise."

"That's good enough for me," he said. "I'll start a preliminary investigation on this embezzlement business, and then bring you up to speed when you're ready."

I knew right at that moment that I couldn't have asked for a better boss. He was giving me all the time I needed for a successful outcome.

"Any word?" Conor said as he brushed away the loose hairs on the back of Eugene's neck.

"I hope to have some news for you real soon," I said.

"If there's anything I can do to help, you let me know," Conor said.

I did need his help—and Eugene's—but I was hesitant to ask for it. Would it be cheating, I wondered, to ask for a little advice? Again? When Eugene first gave me the case, he had said that if ever I needed any assistance, he'd be glad to provide it. I had already bothered him once. I hoped he wouldn't mind another question or two. There was only one way to find out.

"Actually, I did have a question I wanted to bounce off both of you."

"Fire away," Conor said.

Eugene sat up in his chair. He appeared interested.

"I was wondering if there were any farms in the area."

Conor and Eugene looked quizzically at each other.

"Now, why would you want to know that?" Eugene asked.

"Well, we have evidence that the birds might have been taken to a farm," I said.

Conor set his scissors down and folded his arms.

"What kind of evidence?" Eugene asked.

I was hesitant to tell Eugene everything I knew. I was afraid that if he sensed danger, he would either want to take over the investigation himself, or want me off the case for my own safety.

"Just a gut feeling," I said.

"If you're destined to become a successful P.I. someday, Charlie, you're gonna need more than *a gut feeling*. You need physical evidence—hard evidence. Acting on your instincts can appear to be the right thing to do—I've done it a few times successfully—and paid dearly for it other times. Remember, it's always more prudent to let the *evidence* determine your next move. Got it?"

I just stood there. I wasn't sure what to say.

Eugene stood up and yanked the cape from around his neck. "Please tell me you're not getting in over your head here. I know this is your case and all, but if you need a little expert advice, you'd better come clean now. Tell me what you've got. I may be able to help. The sooner we wrap this thing up, the sooner you can do some real detective work."

I felt my shoulders slump. It suddenly made no sense withholding information from my boss. I decided to just spit it out.

"Henry and I saw this kid sell some dead birds to a woman in a pickup truck last night. When she pulled away, we found some hay on the ground. We just figured it had to have come from a farm or something."

"Whoa, whoa, whoa, whoa, whoa." Eugene held up his hands. "Let's start from the top. Who's *Henry*? Someone else knows about all of this?"

"I wanted to tell you, Eugene. He's my best friend. We've been solving cases together for years. It just didn't seem right leaving him out."

Eugene turned and rubbed the back of his neck. He didn't appear happy. "Didn't I ask you not to tell anyone?"

"I know. I'm sorry. But Henry's cool. He won't say a word. And Grandma thought it would be okay to tell him. As a matter of fact, you've probably seen him around. He comes to the library sometimes . . . well, actually, not a lot. He's not a big reader. But if you got to know him, you'd like him."

"Let's get back to the case." Eugene pointed his finger at me. "Just don't tell anyone else. A good P.I. only shares his findings with his partner and his client. Got it?"

"I know. I'm sorry. I won't tell another soul. You can trust me this time. I promise."

Eugene sat back down in the barber chair. Conor retied the cape around his neck.

"Okay, now tell me about this kid who sold the birds."

"His name is Sherman Doyle. I go to school with him. We followed him last night. We saw him kidnap a bunch of birds from a pet store. Then he met up with this woman in a pickup and made the drop."

"Are you positive the birds were dead?" Conor asked.

"Well, they sure looked that way. He just poured them out of a bag. They didn't move a feather."

Conor appeared bothered by the news. "Do me a favor," he said. "Don't tell Scarlett. Socrates was up in years but it's hard to imagine he's gone. Okay?"

"Okay."

"What did this woman in the pickup look like?" Eugene said.

"She was big and tall and wide . . . and ugly. I still can't get that face out of my head."

"And she just drove off with the birds?" Eugene asked.

"Yep."

"And what about the other guy—the kid?"

"He took off. We didn't bother to follow him after that."

Conor picked up his scissors. "So you think that's what's been happening to all the birds around here?"

"That's my guess."

"I don't get it," Conor said. "What do you do with a dead bird? And who'd want to pay for it?"

"I just got a feeling . . . if we can find this farm, everything will make sense," I said. "Are there any around here?"

Conor reflected for a moment. "There's gotta be a half-dozen farms north and west of here, I think."

"That sounds about right," Eugene said, nodding.

"Are any of them owned by a woman?" I asked.

"None come to mind," Conor said. "Can you think of any, Eugene?"

"I don't believe so."

Conor put his finger to his lips. "Now, if that description you gave was for a *man*, then I could tell you exactly where to look. Rupert Olsen's farm—out on Route Thirty-four."

Eugene rose from the chair with a serious look on

his face. "I'd really prefer if you kids stayed away from there. It could be dangerous."

"He *is* a little creepy," Conor said.

"A little?" Eugene snapped. "Do me a favor. Just steer clear."

Eugene had piqued my curiosity. "What is it about this guy that bothers you?" I asked.

"A lot of folks have had run-ins with him," Eugene ·said. "Heck, he's been in jail a half-dozen times."

"For what?" The more I learned about this Rupert Olsen, the more interesting he became.

"Disturbing the peace. Resisting arrest. Theft. He's just a bad egg."

"How does a farmer get into trouble like that?" I said.

"That's just it," Conor replied. "He lives on a farm, but I don't think he's actually a farmer. He's had all kinds of jobs. Long-haul trucker, janitor, locksmith."

"Locksmith? Right! Till he got arrested and lost his license," Eugene said.

"Yeah, he's worn a lot of hats, but farmer isn't one of 'em," Conor said. "If you drive by his property, you won't see anything growing in his fields."

"I still occasionally see a couple of dairy cows out there," Eugene added. He looked me square in the eye. "I want you to promise me you'll stay away from there, you got it?"

"Okay," I said. But I wasn't sure if I really meant it.

How could I make a promise like that? What if our investigation pointed squarely at this culprit? It would be my obligation to check it out.

Just then Scarlett entered the shop. "Hi, everybody."

"Hi, sweetie," her grandfather said.

"So, Charlie, got any news for me?" she said.

Conor glanced in my direction. His body language suggested that I steer clear of certain issues. I was happy to oblige.

"We have reason to believe that a kid at school may be the birdnapper."

"Really? Who?"

I wasn't sure if I should rat out Sherman yet. It was best if he didn't know we were on to him, and if Scarlett freaked out and confronted him, who knew what might happen.

"I don't have a name yet. But I'm working on it."

"Shouldn't we be taking this to the police?"

"We need more evidence."

"Is that it?" she asked.

"There's more. It appears that this kid hands over the birds to an unidentified woman, and then they're transported to a farm in the area, we think."

Eugene interrupted. "I don't care what your theory is, Charlie, but if you're thinking of visiting certain places around here, remember what we talked about." Eugene raised his eyebrows.

The room became very quiet.

"What's with all the mystery?" Scarlett said. "You make it sound kind of scary."

"And that's just what I'm trying to do," Eugene said.

I turned to Scarlett and pointed at the door. "Why don't we go for a walk? I'll fill you in on a few things."

"Okay."

"Hey, kids," Eugene said as we were about to leave. "I want to know exactly what your plans are *before* you actually carry them out. Got it?"

"Got it." I waved to both gentlemen as we left.

As Scarlett and I walked, I was silent. I was trying to find a way to tell her what we had seen the night before. Part of me wanted to spare her the pain of hearing that Socrates might be dead. But I also felt that since she was a paying client, it wouldn't be professional not to share all the information we had found. I decided at that moment that she had to know, and it was my obligation to tell her.

"You said you were going to fill me in," she said. "What else is there?"

"I just thought you should know that there's a likelihood that we may never find your grandpa's bird . . . or any of the missing birds. They might be out of the state . . . or out of the country for that matter. I don't want you to get your hopes up."

"Back there you said that someone was taking them to a farm in the area."

"That's possible, but who knows what happens to them after that?"

"Then why don't we go over to this farm before it's too late?"

"Well, we don't know which farm it is. There's more than one."

"Then let's check all of them," she suggested.

"I suppose we could do that."

"You suppose? Isn't that the next logical step?"

"It's certainly one of the options we need to consider," I said. I know she's the client, but it's my case. I get to call the shots. She should know that.

"Then why can't we just go over there?" Scarlett said. "Is there some problem?"

"I don't want to rush into anything," I said. I was trying to do everything in my power to spare her a little grief. The last thing I wanted to do was to march over to one of those farms and find a bunch of dead birds. There was no reason to put her through that. How could I make her see this without coming right out and saying that Socrates was probably history?

Or was I trying to spare *myself* a little grief? This whole lost-bird thing seemed like something I should have been able to handle in a relatively safe fashion. But I didn't like the way Eugene had described this Rupert Olsen character. He sounded like one scary dude. I was hoping that he had nothing to do with any of this. But the more I thought about it, the more I had myself convinced that he might be involved. He owned a farm. We had found hay. Although he was a man, he matched the description that Eugene and Conor had given me. And Olsen had a record. This made him a likely suspect. I just couldn't tie him to the crime, but I had a bad feeling I would eventually come face-to-face with him.

And if I was right, and if he *was* somehow involved, I wasn't so sure I was willing to tangle with him. What had I gotten myself into? I was beginning to rethink my decision to take on this case. Impressing Scarlett was one thing—but placing yourself in harm's way was another. Was there a way to back out and still save face?

"Are you afraid to go out to this farm?" she said. "Is that it?"

"Afraid? Right."

"Then what am I paying you for anyway? And you never told me how much all of this is going to cost."

Ouch! That one hurt. But the worst part was that she was right. I wasn't earning my fee—whatever that was. If I could just tie this old woman to one particular farm, then I'd have it. I thought back to last night. Had I missed something? Was there an obvious clue staring me in the face? Maybe it was time to bring the latest note to Grandma. I tried to replay everything we had seen in the prairie the night before. There was Sherman . . . the sack . . . the dead birds . . . the pickup truck . . . the old woman . . . the *mammoth* old woman . . . the red lipstick . . . the mysterious note . . . the trench coat.

Something about that trench coat still bothered me. I knew there was something odd about it . . . but what? It wasn't the color. And it seemed to fit her okay, although it wasn't what you'd call feminine. No, there was something else. The buttons maybe? I tried to re-create the image of this massive old woman in a trench coat. Something just wasn't right. What was it? I was stalling—hoping that lightning would strike—hoping that a pearl of wisdom would miraculously appear. And then it suddenly hit me. It *was* the buttons. Why hadn't I thought of it before? It was buttoned on the wrong side. Women button their coats on the left side. Hers was buttoned on the right. That was it!

"Then *she's* gotta be a *he*," I blurted out.

"What are you talking about?"

"The old woman's not a woman. She's a man. *She* . . . I mean, *he's* just trying to throw us off his trail . . . *and* . . . I know exactly who took the birds—and where they are. Well, not exactly. I don't have an address or anything, but I know the general area."

"Well, let's go," she said.

"It's not quite that easy. We can't just barge in there. I need to discuss it with my partner first."

"Your partner? You mean Eugene?" she said.

I wasn't sure she was ready to hear this, but she'd find out sooner or later. "No, not Eugene. I'm talking about Henry."

Scarlett threw her head back. She wasn't pleased. "Henry? You're kidding, right?"

I avoided eye contact. "No, I've asked him to join us on the case."

"Why does he have to help? We don't need him."

"Listen, if you really want to find Socrates, if you care about him as much as you say, then you have to understand that we stand a much better chance *with* Henry than *without* him." There. I'd said it. I'd thrown it back in her court. What could she say now? She had to buy into the plan.

"You *are* afraid to go to this farm, aren't you?"

"What are you talking about? I'm not afraid of anything. I just think that arming oneself with the proper personnel is the only way to guarantee a successful mission."

"So, what's waiting for us at this farmhouse that's got you so nervous?"

She just wouldn't quit. I had half a mind to tell her everything. That'd show her.

"Maybe I'll just go over there myself," she said.

"And come face-to-face with a killer—is that what you want to do?" I couldn't help myself.

"A killer?"

"Listen, we figure that the birds were taken to a farm. And I think that the farm in question is owned by one Rupert Olsen, who Henry and I just happened to see drive off with a bunch of *dead* birds."

"Dead?"

I was sorry I had said it, but it was too late. "Yes, dead."

"I don't believe it. I don't believe you saw anything like that. I think you're just trying to scare me into backing out of this whole thing. You're just afraid to go over there."

This girl had become completely unreasonable. Was this the same Scarlett Alexander who for the last several years had made me weak in the knees? Had she gone completely nuts?

I knew that I'd been whining about wanting a shot at the big score for years, but did she really expect me to just march up to some lowlife and ask him if he was the one behind the missing birds? The dead birds? There was no reason to take that risk. We just needed to wait it out, scare up some new evidence, analyze our findings, and if it took a few weeks, so be it.

I took a deep breath. The more I listened to my own reasoning, the more I realized that she was right. I was uneasy about meeting up with this character. I *was* afraid. I didn't like the feeling. When Eugene told me that this mystery man had been in and out of jail,

I should have been salivating. This was exciting stuff. Instead I was sweating. I began to rethink what I really wanted out of life. Was I going to freeze every time danger presented itself? I never thought I'd react that way. Over the years, I had myself convinced that if I was ever fortunate enough to find myself embroiled in the type of case found on the pages of a Sam Solomon novel, I'd be in my glory.

Maybe I'd been fooling myself all along. Maybe I should have been satisfied with the measly mysteries I was able to solve from the comfort of my garage. Nothing dangerous about that.

But I did know one thing—even if this case proved perilous, and even if I decided to abandon the big score in the future, I knew that I had to honor my commitment. I had taken on a client. I had promised results. And I had to see it through, no matter what.

"All right, then," I said. "Tomorrow—I'll meet you in front of your grandpa's shop at about nine o'clock—nine o'clock at night, that is. And we'll go check out that farm for ourselves."

"*We'll* go check it out? Why do you need me?"

"Just a minute ago, you said you were gonna go over there yourself. Do you want to go or not?"

"Well, I only said that because you seemed too scared to do it alone."

"Now who's the scared one?" It was a cheap shot, I know, but it had to be said.

Scarlett needed to digest that thought for a moment. She seemed uncertain of what to do.

"I guess . . . I guess I'll meet you there tomorrow night then," she said.

"Can I really count on you showing up?"

"I'll be there," she snapped.

"You should know—I'm bringing Henry along."

"Oh, I can hardly wait," she said sarcastically.

CHAPTER 12

The Poultry in Motion Caper

On Saturday morning, Henry stopped over at the house and we made one last attempt at decoding the note. We tried every possible combination of letters and numbers we could think of. Nothing made any sense. And if that wasn't bad enough, we still didn't know where we were headed tonight. If Scarlett's grandpa was right about there being a half-dozen farms in the area, how could we possibly know which one was the Olsen farm? I supposed we'd have to visit all of them just to be sure. That could take all night. And what if we got caught? Would they charge us with trespassing and lock us up? This whole thing was starting to sound like a very bad idea.

"Why don't we just ask Eugene where this farm is?" Henry said.

"Like he's gonna tell us," I said. "He made it very clear that we were to stay away from there. He'd never divulge the location, trust me."

"You got a phone book?" Henry asked. "Maybe Olsen's in there."

Why hadn't I thought of that? Sometimes I get myself so caught up in a case that I miss the obvious. I ran downstairs to the living room and found the phone book buried under some magazines. I raced back to my room.

"Got it," I said. I opened it up to the *O*s and began searching for Olsen's name. We soon found more names than we were expecting.

"There's Olson with an *o* and Olsen with an *e*," Henry said. "Which one is it?"

"I don't know," I said. "Let's see if we can figure it out from the addresses." I knew that a farm would have to have a rural address of some kind. It wouldn't be a normal street or avenue or lane or anything like that. A minute or so later, we were back at square one.

"All of these addresses are in town," Henry said. "I recognize most of the streets. Olsen must be unlisted."

"So now what?" I said.

"We could go on the Internet and search for him that way," Henry suggested.

I slammed the phone book shut. "Absolutely not," I said. Henry just didn't get it. Sam Solomon had no problem tracking down leads long before the Internet ever existed. If I was forced to use new technology to solve a case, I'd feel like I had cheated.

"Just a suggestion," he said. "But if you want to do it the hard way, it's fine with me."

I sat on the bed and stewed for a minute. I was determined to figure this out with the same tools that Sam had used.

"Let's just put this on the back burner for now," Henry said. "Why don't we go ask your grandma to help us decipher that note we found? Then we'll worry about locating the farm later. Okay? We're running out of time, Charlie."

I sighed. I hated having to ask for help again. I really wanted to figure this one out by myself, but Henry was right. Time was now the enemy.

"I guess so," I said reluctantly. "Let's find her."

We did a quick search of the house. No Grandma. My mom was in the kitchen cleaning up after breakfast.

"Mom, do you know were Gram is?"

"The Pocono Five Hundred," she said with a smirk.

"Huh?"

"Look in the garage," she said.

When we found Gram, she was sitting behind the steering wheel of the minivan wearing a helmet and dressed in full racing attire. She rolled the window down and stuck her head out.

"Hey, Johnson, you ain't got nothing," Grandma yelled out. "You drive like an old lady." She then proceeded to turn the wheel back and forth in an animated fashion and made engine sounds with her mouth. "*Vroom, vroom.*"

I was a little uncertain about interrupting her, especially in the middle of a race. But we were on deadline.

"Gram, can we bother you for a minute?"

She looked in our direction. "Gotta make a pit stop anyway. Watch your toes, boys." She turned the wheel toward us and made a screeching sound. *"Errrrrr."* She climbed out of the window feetfirst and landed with a thud on the garage floor. "Fill 'er up, gents," she yelled out to her imaginary crew. "You got thirty seconds, fellas," she said to us, "and no autographs."

I reached into my pocket for the note and handed it to her. "We need your help again."

She grinned. She seemed to enjoy playing this little game. The note said:

11-24-12-18   11-24-12-18
16-24-12-14-7
14-7-18-13-13   26-5-26-13   14-7-18-13-13
18-24-12-14-13   14-7-18-13-13   11-24-12-18

"We tried to decode it ourselves, Mrs. Collier," Henry said. "But we just couldn't figure it out."

As Gram studied the note, her expression turned serious. And then just as quickly, she was smiling again. "It's similar to the last one, but this time it's backward."

"How do you mean?" I asked.

"Well, the letter *k* is still the number one. Then this

fellow went backward and added two—so the *j* is a 3—and he did so all the way to the beginning of the alphabet." She paused momentarily and studied the note. "Then he seems to have assigned the number two to the letter *z*. And likewise went backward adding two at a time and ending with the letter *l*." She held up the note. "Do you see? This code is actually much simpler than the last one."

I understood the pattern but was amazed at how quickly she had figured it out.

"So what's this one say?" Henry asked.

"Looks like another address, but this time he spelled out the numbers," Gram said. "Let's see now: Four four . . . South . . . Three nine three . . . Route Three Four." She smiled. "Forty-four South Three Ninety-three Route Thirty-four."

"Where's that?" Henry said.

"Clear as I can tell, it's about three miles north of town in an unincorporated area."

"What's over there?" I asked.

"It's all farmland. This is probably the address of a farmhouse."

Henry poked me in the ribs and nodded. He was thinking the same thing I was. This was the address we'd been looking for. Olsen had written down the location of his farmhouse and given it to Sherman that night. It all made sense. Maybe that would be the next drop-off site. And all of this had been served up and handed to us on a plate by Grandma. In less than a minute, she had managed to decipher the mystery note *and* had pinpointed the location of the farm all in one motion. She was something else, all right.

Gram handed the note back to me. "Well, gotta run, gentlemen." She climbed headfirst through the window and back into the driver's seat. She stuck her head out and looked back. "We ready to go, Smitty?" She smiled, waved to her crew and sped off. "*Vroom, vroom.*"

We spent the remainder of the day planning out our course of action. All the while I was feeling a little guilty about deceiving Eugene. But I knew that if I informed him of our intentions to pay Mr. Olsen a visit tonight, he would never allow it. I figured that if we found what we were looking for, he'd be okay with it after the fact. At least, I hoped so.

I was also feeling pretty guilty about the lies that Henry and I had told our parents. We each had said that we were sleeping over at the other's house tonight. We were praying that our moms never got wise and decided to check up on us. But we didn't want to have a curfew hanging over our heads. There was no telling what we were in for. It was best not to have someone waiting up for us.

We left the house after dinner and went over to Henry's for a while. We thought it best to make appearances at both locations. At about eight fifteen, we hopped on our bikes and headed out. We arrived at our destination a couple of minutes before nine o'clock. The only light on at the barber shop when we arrived was the red-and-white pole in front. Scarlett was running late. We parked our bikes in the doorway and sat down on the front steps.

"So, I never asked you—what did Scarlett say when you told her I was joining the team?" Henry said.

"To be honest, I don't recall."

He grinned. "Your nose is growing, Charlie."

I knew he'd never believe me.

"It doesn't matter," he said. "We've worked with difficult clients before. You don't gotta like 'em. It's just business."

I smiled.

"Then again," he said. "When Scarlett sees me in action, things could change. Who knows?"

I chuckled.

A few minutes later, Scarlett rode up. We stood to greet her. Henry made the mistake of glancing at his watch. She took it the wrong way.

"I got caught by a freight train," she said. "Is that all right with you?"

Henry shook his head. He was taking the high road. At least he was trying.

"Well, are we ready to roll?" I said.

"I still don't see why you need me," Scarlett said.

"I thought you wanted to be along for the kill," I said.

"Do you always put your clients to work?"

Henry stepped between us. The gloves were now off. The truce hadn't lasted long.

"Let me tell you something, Scarlett. I don't really care if you come with us or not. As a matter of fact, now that I've had time to think about it, I'd prefer that you didn't. We don't usually offer the client an opportunity to tag along. We were extending you a rare privilege. You can take it or leave it."

Scarlett glared at Henry, then at me. "This is why I didn't want him here," she said.

"Listen," I said. "I just thought that maybe you wanted to help find the people who might have stolen your grandfather's bird. And if we somehow find him, then you'd be right there to ID Socrates for us."

"Well, you certainly know what a parrot looks like," she said. "I don't see what the big deal is."

"So does that mean you won't be tagging along?" Henry said with a smirk.

"That's just what you'd like, isn't it?" she said.

"I can think of nothing better."

"Okay then, in that case . . . I'm in."

Henry wasn't expecting that answer. And all I could think about was having to referee this verbal sparring match all night. It wasn't going to be pleasant.

"This whole thing can't end soon enough as far as I'm concerned," she said.

"For me too," Henry echoed.

Someone had to defuse this situation. And it certainly wasn't going to be either of them.

"Guys," I said. "Let's just do what we came here to do. Let's go find these birds, return them to their owners, and let's try to be civil to one another. Okay?"

I held up my flashlight. "Henry, got yours?"

Henry held his up.

"Scarlett?"

Scarlett checked her jeans pockets, then her jacket pockets. No flashlight.

"Sorry," she said. "But I do have this." She held up her cell phone. "Don't you have one?"

"No," I said. "I don't need one. If Sam Solomon was able to unravel countless mysteries in the *pre*-cell phone days, I can certainly do the same."

"And I don't have one because my parents live in the Dark Ages and they won't let me get one until I'm in high school—but if I could have one, I would. Does that answer your question?" Henry said.

Scarlett looked at us as if we were both nuts.

With that, we hopped onto our metal steeds and headed north to the city limits. We rode our bikes in a single file. I assumed the lead and attempted to maintain a steady pace throughout the trek. There were moments when fatigue kicked in, and I wanted to pull over. Instead I just slowed down a little. Henry and Scarlett never said a word when I seemed to labor up steep inclines. We traveled down side streets, alleys, through open prairies, and at times, thick brush. We had checked a local map and knew we were headed to a farmstead at the intersection of Route 34 and Prospect Road. It was nearly 9:40 when we reached our destination.

A six-foot chain-link fence surrounded the Olsen farm. It was a little hard to see in the dark but we could certainly make out a string of barbed wire running across the top. We abandoned our bikes and walked along the perimeter of the property in hopes of finding an entrance of some kind. Within a few minutes, we came across metal gates. An oversize padlock and a thick metal chain held them tightly together.

"Now what?" Scarlett said. "There's no way to get in. We may as well go back."

Henry chuckled.

I aimed my flashlight in his direction. "What's so funny?"

"I can't believe the master of mystery, Charlie Collier, Snoop for Hire, would have left home without these." Henry pulled a small handheld pair of wire cutters from his pocket.

It was a friendly dig, but I was okay with it. Henry began to cut a hole in the fence.

"Wait a minute. You can't just damage someone's property like that," Scarlett said.

"Just whose side are you on?" Henry said.

"What do you mean?"

"We're doing all of this to help find your grandpa's bird," Henry replied. "I can justify it."

Scarlett sighed. "This is all so creepy. And I'm scared. Okay, is that what you want to hear?!"

I was scared too but I couldn't let on. Henry busily cut his way through the wire fencing. He paid no attention to us.

"Okay, see if you can squeeze through here," he said.

Henry had bent back some of the metal ends so we wouldn't catch our clothes as we climbed through. I didn't want to say anything, but at that moment, I sure wished I was lean and mean. There was no way I'd fit through that hole.

"I'll go first," Henry said. And with that, he slithered through. "Who's next?"

"Ladies first," I said to Scarlett.

"If you don't mind, I'll go last. I still haven't decided if I'm doing this or not."

A flapping sound overhead caught our attention.

"What was that?" she said.

"That was a bat," Henry announced.

Scarlett suddenly made her mind up rather quickly. She dropped to all fours and crawled through.

Now what? I could easily see that the hole wasn't nearly big enough for me to squeeze through. But I couldn't just say "I can't fit." I smiled nervously at Henry. He returned a friendly grin. I tried to communicate to him with my eyes. Please, friend, help me save face here. I swallowed and took a deep breath. Anything to delay the inevitable. I glanced at Henry one more time. He motioned for me to come through.

Then all at once, as if someone had magically whispered something into his ear, he reached into his pocket for the wire cutters and bent down.

"You know, Charlie, I think your jacket is gonna catch on one of these sharp ends. Let me tweak it a little." He proceeded to cut through several more wires. As he snipped, he looked up at me and winked. He had read my body language—the way only a best friend could. A moment later, I slipped through and joined the others.

We pointed our flashlights in various directions until they locked onto a farmhouse in the distance.

"That's gotta be it," I said. "Let's do this thing."

The grass was thick and wet. We took large, high steps to maneuver our way through it.

"Oh great!" Henry yelled. He lifted his foot and shined his flashlight on the bottom of his shoe.

"What? What is it?" Scarlett said.

"I stepped on a cow pie," Henry said disgustedly.

"A cow pie? What's that?"

"Look real close . . . and smell."

Scarlett leaned in. Henry and I laughed at the same time.

"Oh God, that is so gross," she said.

"It's all about nature," Henry said. "Cows have urges too, you know."

Scarlett lifted her foot and attempted to look at the bottom of her shoe. "Can I borrow a flashlight, please?" she said.

"Why don't you use your cell phone?" Henry said, trying to contain his laughter. He was unsuccessful.

"Very funny." Scarlett reached into her pocket to retrieve her phone. Then another pocket. It was gone. "My phone! It's gone! It must have fallen out when we were riding over some of those bumps. I have to find it!"

"You'll never find it out here," Henry said. "It's a goner."

Scarlett shook her head and snarled. "This is a bad idea. This whole thing is a very bad idea."

Henry wiped his foot on some tall grass and shook his head. He was still chuckling.

"Well, I'm glad you enjoyed that," she said.

"Let's just get back to work." I pointed at the farmhouse. "Come on."

We stepped quietly but carefully as we proceeded. From our vantage point, we could see a faint light on the first floor. We moved closer and hid behind a tree about fifty yards away.

"Why don't the two of you stay here for a minute. I wanna see something," I said.

"Nothing doin'," Henry said. "We're a team."

"You're not leaving me here alone," Scarlett squealed.

The three of us crouched down and crept toward the back of the house.

It was an old structure, built in the 1930s, I'd guess. As we got closer we could see that it was in pretty shabby condition. Paint peeled from every surface. The window screens were falling off. We didn't exactly know what we were looking for. When Henry tripped over an empty pail, we soon found out.

"Oh man, that hurt," he said as he climbed to his feet.

"Wait a minute. Did you hear something?" I said.

"I didn't hear anything," Scarlett replied.

I pointed at a cellar door a few feet away. "It came from over there, I'm sure of it."

We tiptoed to the door and immediately knew we had hit the jackpot. The squawking was unmistakable.

Henry's eyes lit up. "There's a bunch of birds down there."

"Do you think Socrates is in there?" Scarlett asked. She looked hopeful.

"Only one way to find out," I said. "Come on."

The cellar door was one of the old types that had

to be lifted straight up. We yanked on it but it wouldn't budge. A metal chain had been snaked through the door handles, and a padlock held it in place.

"Oh great!" I said. "Now what?"

"Boy, you've got a short memory," Henry said as he pulled the wire cutters from his back pocket.

"This chain's thicker than that fence back there," I said. "Think you can get through it?"

"Piece of cake," Henry answered. He knelt down, clamped the wire cutters onto the chain, and squeezed. A series of grunts and an occasional sigh followed. As he struggled, it seemed for a moment there that Henry had met his match. I held the flashlight directly over his head. Even with the dim lighting, we could see Henry's face reddening.

"I'm gettin' there," he said.

And with one last two-handed squeeze, Henry let out a loud, long groan, and . . . *SNAP!* He had done it. We pulled the remaining piece of chain out from under the handles and lifted the cellar doors. When we had opened it just a crack, the screeching sounds got noticeably louder.

"Who's coming with me?" I asked.

"I'm in," Henry said.

"Me too, I guess," Scarlett said. "I'm not staying out here alone."

We threw open the door and proceeded down a set

of stone stairs. The squawking and fluttering was deafening. As soon as we stepped onto the cement floor, and aimed our flashlights forward, we knew we had hit pay dirt. The room was filled with cages from end to end. I spotted an overhead light and flipped it on.

Henry slapped me on the back. "Eureka!" he said. "Now let's find that bird and get the heck out of here."

"All right. Henry, you stay here by the door and listen. We'll go look for Socrates."

We'd been at it only a few minutes when I noticed Henry waving his arms.

"I thought I heard something," he whispered.

A second later, Scarlett let out a blood-curdling scream that scared me half to death.

"Look!" she shrieked. She pointed to a tiny window up near the ceiling. There was a large, grotesque face staring back at us. Whoever it was seemed to be smiling.

"C'mon, let's get out of here," I yelled.

The next sound was the one I was dreading—the sound of the cellar doors being slammed shut.

"Who was that?" Scarlett cried.

It had to be Rupert Olsen. Who else could it be? We could hear him trying to pull what was left of the chain through the door handles. He seemed to struggle with it at first—and then we heard a *click*. He had somehow managed to slip the padlock through the ends of the shortened chain.

Henry ran up the stairs and pounded on the heavy wooden door. It wouldn't budge. We quickly searched for another exit. Nothing. Even the windows had been boarded up. We glanced at the window where we had seen the face. It was now covered.

"We're trapped!" Scarlett screamed.

I sprinted up the stairs and threw my body at the cellar doors. All I got for my effort was a bruised shoulder.

"Let us out of here!" I yelled. I could hear movement outside. "I think he's still out there," I told the others. And then my suspicions were confirmed.

"You're not goin' anywhere right now," a muffled voice said. "And don't touch anything. If you do, you'll be sorry."

We could hear laughter and footsteps trailing off.

"We *are* trapped," Henry said.

Scarlett was now standing at the bottom of the stairs. She was wiping her eyes. "What's gonna happen to us now?" she whimpered.

I tried to seem calm. "We'll just have to wait for somebody to find us," I said.

"And if they don't?" Scarlett said.

"Well, I don't know exactly. But we'll figure something out."

"We can't just wait until some madman comes back," Scarlett said. "Maybe if we all screamed, someone would hear us."

"Are you kidding?!" Henry said. "We couldn't hear those birds until we were right on top of this place."

I knew that the prudent thing to do would be to resolve this problem ourselves—to break out of here. I also knew that I was the one who needed to map out a strategy—an escape plan of some sort. I kept waiting for an idea to pop into my head. The longer I waited, the more my brain fizzled. There was just no way out of this place. Period. My only thought—the window—was far too high up, and even then, much too small—even for Henry to wiggle through. We found a dry spot in the corner and plopped down. I sat and waited for inspiration to hit.

It was starting to get late. And the worst part of all was that no one would be looking for us. Our folks thought Henry and I were at each other's house. Even Scarlett had made up a story about a sleepover with a friend. We were on our own. We huddled together to stay warm. No one spoke for several minutes but we all knew what the other was thinking or, rather, dreading. And I also knew that the others would be expecting *me* to come up with an escape plan. It only made sense. I was the one who prided myself on being able to solve even the most challenging brainteasers.

So now I had finally gotten my wish—the big score—and a real-life brainteaser to boot. I needed to stop panicking and start brainstorming. I needed to think like Sam Solomon. In nearly every one of his novels,

Sam had been held captive at one time or another. Which Sam Solomon story would apply here? I created a mental picture of the bookshelf in my bedroom. I thought carefully about each story—and then it hit me. Of course—Episode #17—*The Poultry in Motion Caper.* There were birds in that story—just like here. I traced the plot in my head. I kept waiting for something to jump out—something that would assist us in our escape. But all I could think about was Rupert Olsen, and what he had planned for us when he returned. I was scared. I rolled up into a ball. I was ashamed of myself. And then I realized that there *was* a similarity between this particular Sam Solomon case and our situation. Both stories had chickens in them.

CHAPTER 13

The Hits and Mrs. Caper

A good hour had passed and still nothing. Scarlett had examined all of the cages. Socrates was nowhere in sight. We sat quietly for several minutes. No one spoke. Henry eventually broke the ice.

"Okay, Charlie, imagine this: There are these two boxers in a boxing match . . ."

"A riddle? You expect me to solve a riddle at a time like this? I'm trying to think of a way out of this place if you don't mind."

"I just figured this would get your brain cooking. C'mon, try it. See, there's these two boxers in a boxing match. It's scheduled to go twelve rounds, but one boxer knocks out the other one in the sixth round. But no man ever threw a punch. How's it possible?"

It seemed crazy to be tackling a brain buster after some psycho had locked us up in this hole, but maybe Henry was right. Maybe I needed to jump-start the old noodle. Let me see now.

"What are you two talking about?" Scarlett asked.

"Shhhh," Henry said. "He's thinking."

"Thinking about some brainteaser? He should be thinking about how we can get out of this place," she snapped.

I repeated the details. "Two boxers. Twelve rounds. It ended after six rounds. But no one threw a punch."

"That's right," Henry said. "No man ever threw a punch."

"Say that again," I said.

"What do you mean?"

"That last part."

"No man ever threw a punch."

Of course. I listened to the way that Henry had rephrased what I had said. He went out of his way to replace *no one* with *no man*—and there lay the answer.

"No man ever threw a punch," I announced, "because they were women boxers." I tried to make it seem as though I had solved this one thanks to my amazing powers of deduction but I really had to thank Sam Solomon. In Episode #4—*The Hits and Mrs. Caper*— Sam exposed a crooked fight promoter who was fixing matches—matches fought by none other than female boxers.

Henry clenched his fists and groaned. "Before I die, Collier, I'm gonna stump you. Just wait."

"Well, then give him some more," Scarlett blurted

out, "because we're probably all gonna be dead soon." Her patience had run out. "And let me tell you something, Charlie—you really blew it. You couldn't find Socrates, and now we're all prisoners because of you."

I winced and looked down, ashamed. I wanted to defend myself in the worst way but she was right. I had really screwed this up. I wasn't quite sure what to say. Should I apologize? Should I tell her everything was going to be all right? Should I remind her that Sam Solomon got into scrapes like these all of the time . . . and always managed to escape? I considered my options.

"Listen, Scarlett," I said. "I know that things look a little bleak—"

Henry held his hand up. "Wait a second. Did you hear that?"

There was a sound—a strange, high-pitched voice coming from across the cellar.

"Scarlett," the voice said.

She turned in the direction of the sound. "What was that?"

"Scarlett. I . . . love . . . you," the voice said.

And with that, we all ran in the direction of the sound. It appeared to be coming from a room hidden behind one of the large cages.

"There's somebody in there," I said. "Come on, Henry, help me move this out of the way."

We slid the cage back and entered the room. I flipped

on my flashlight. The space was small and had a damp smell. On the far wall was a shelf with more cages. I moved the light over each one, then stopped abruptly.

"Socrates!" Scarlett screamed. "It's you. You're okay." She ran over, lifted the cage, and hugged it.

We were just about to leave when I sensed that we weren't alone. Something, I feared, was standing directly between my legs. When I moved the flashlight down and saw the fattest rat I had ever seen, I bolted out of the room and into the cellar.

"Get out of my way!" Henry yelled as he pushed past us.

"Ahhhhh!" Scarlett screamed and scooted out, but managed to catch her jacket on a hook attached to the door frame. She pulled at it but couldn't break free. The more she tried to undo it, the more tangled it became. "Charlie, help me!"

The hook had ripped through the outside of her jacket and was clinging tightly to the inside lining. Scarlett's repeated attempts to unhook herself weren't helping any. I needed to bend the hook downward. Maybe then we could slide the jacket off. When I pushed down on the hook, I heard a sound. It was like a motor of some sort. And before our eyes, a wall began to slide open, revealing another room.

Henry ran back over. Scarlett's jacket was now free. And the three of us just stared into the room that had been hidden moments before. We glanced at one another. We couldn't believe what we were seeing. There were more birds—dozens of them. But no squawking this time. And none of them were in cages. Each one was sitting upright on a perch, with its head cocked to one side. The perches were supported by a metal base with a nameplate on the front of each one, and words engraved on it. We crept into the room and began reading some of them.

"Look at this one," Scarlett said, as she read aloud, "'American peregrine falcon.'"

"Why does that sound familiar?" Henry said.

The name *was* familiar. But where had I heard it? Had I seen something on TV? Had I read it in a book? No, wait a minute. It was in school, I think. Yeah. It was Mrs. Jansen's class. Of course, that was it.

"That bird's on the endangered species list," I said. "Remember? About a week ago in science class?"

"You're right," Henry said. "And didn't she say that one of these falcons was missing from a wildlife sanctuary?"

"I guess he's not missing anymore," I said.

Henry pointed at another nameplate that read NORTHERN SPOTTED OWL. "This one's on the list too."

The entire room was filled with birds. Dead birds. Stuffed birds. There were parrots, cockatoos, macaws, cockatiels, hawks, pelicans, egrets, buzzards, you name it. And off to the side was a table with what could only be described as . . . bird parts.

"What's going on here?" Scarlett said.

"*I'll* tell you what," Henry said. "This guy's a taxidermist."

"A what?" she said.

"If you're a hunter or a fisherman, a taxidermist is the guy who stuffs the animal for you so you can hang it on your wall. My uncle's got a bunch of these at his house."

"But this guy's not only a taxidermist," I said. "He's a poacher. It's illegal to kill these birds." Then I noticed that some of the stuffed birds had a tag hanging off of them. Each one had a price, a name, and a phone number. "And these must be the buyers."

"This guy's a *black market* taxidermist," Henry said. "Now, wouldn't the authorities just love to get their hands on him?"

I immediately thought about the birds in the cages in the next room. "We can only assume that all the birds out there will eventually end up in here, endangered or not."

"Oh no!" Scarlett cried. "They can't do that to Socrates."

"We gotta save 'em, Charlie. All of 'em," Henry said. "It's our duty."

A scraping sound from outside soon distracted us.

"What was that?" Henry said.

We scrambled out of the room.

"It came from over there," I said.

We moved slowly in the direction of the cellar doors.

There was someone out there, all right. And they were opening the padlock and sliding off the chain.

"I'm afraid," Scarlett said.

I shielded her. "Don't worry."

The door swung open and a bag was dropped onto the cement floor. I couldn't resist. I peeked up, hoping to catch a glimpse of the intruder. The figure was large, but I couldn't quite make out his face. For some crazy reason, I wasn't afraid. I decided it was time to confront the enemy. I aimed my flashlight at him.

"Sherman?" I said.

"Collier?" he yelled as he jumped down into the cellar. "What are you doing here?"

"Somebody locked us up in here. You have to help us get out."

"I don't understand. What's going on?"

Henry decided to set this kid straight. "I'll tell you what's happening. We're trying to save the birds that *you've* been kidnapping . . . and killing."

"Killing? What are you talking about? I'm the one saving these birds."

"What?" Henry said.

"You see all them birds," Sherman said. "They don't belong in cages. It's my job to rescue 'em so they can be shipped back to where they came from and released into the wild. South America. Africa. Places like that."

"Who told you this?" I asked.

He seemed as though he didn't want to answer.

I knelt down and looked into the sack that Sherman had delivered. I pulled out a parrot. It appeared lifeless.

"Did you kill that one too?" Scarlett said.

"Whoa, guys. I didn't kill anybody. He's just asleep . . . kind of. I had to drug him. It didn't hurt him. But some of these buggers put up a pretty good fight." He held up his bandaged hands. "As you can see."

"Sherman, all the birds you've been kidnapping . . . they were bred in captivity, you know." I pointed to the cages. "This is the only life they know. They'd never survive in the wild."

Sherman seemed puzzled.

"You wanna know what's really happening to all these birds?" Henry said.

"What?"

"Come on, I'll show you."

We led Sherman into the back room. When he saw the birds that had been stuffed and mounted, he squeezed the sides of his head. He seemed as if he were trying to keep it from exploding.

"I'm confused," he said.

"Who's paying you to steal these birds?" I asked. "Mr. Olsen?"

I could tell by Sherman's expression that the answer was *yes*.

"I don't know his name. He never told me," Sherman said.

"You didn't know that he kills them, stuffs them, and sells them to collectors, did you?" I said.

Henry picked up the bag and looked inside. "There's at least half a dozen more in here," he said. "I always knew you were bad news, Sherman. This confirms it."

Sherman shook his head, trying to come up with with a response. "Listen, this is the first time I ever did anything like this."

Henry chuckled sarcastically.

"The first time?" I said. "We saw you the other night. In the field? With your boss, Mr. Olsen? He was dressed up like a woman?"

Sherman dropped his head. He seemed embarrassed.

"Why does he do that anyway? Dressing up like that?" Henry said.

"In case somebody saw us out there," Sherman said. "He didn't want anyone to be able to recognize him." Sherman stared at the stuffed birds. There was a pained expression on his face.

"Tell me something," I said. "Why did you bring the birds here this time? Why didn't you just meet up out in that field like before?"

"The old man was getting nervous," Sherman said. "He saw some of the bird stories on TV and in the newspaper. He didn't want to do anything out in the open anymore."

Scarlett approached Sherman. It was almost as if she felt sorry for him.

"You do understand what you did was wrong, don't you?" Scarlett said.

Sherman appeared uneasy. "Listen, I don't know what this guy plans to do with all these birds, but I swear I thought he was letting them go."

I pointed at the stuffed birds all around us. "Doesn't it seem obvious that he has no plans to release them?" I said.

"Sherman," Scarlett said, "why didn't you ask someone before you agreed to do this? Mrs. Jansen at school, for example. If you had asked her about releasing pet birds into the wild, she could have told you that you can't do that. It would be a death sentence for them."

Henry walked to the corner of the room, picked up a stuffed red-tailed hawk, and carried it over.

"Did you catch these big ones too?" he asked.

"No. I don't know anything about them. I was only supposed to take the fancy-colored ones. Olsen hired a bunch of guys. They bring in birds from all over the state." Sherman dropped his head. "I can't believe this. You mean . . . because of me . . . they're all dead?"

I placed my hand on his shoulder. I had never before gotten this close to Sherman without fearing for my life.

"First of all, we have to get out of here. Then we have to make sure that these birds get back to their owners. Can you do that?"

"You're sure about all of this?" he asked.

"Absolutely."

The expression on his face was one I had never seen before. It wasn't that familiar without-a-clue look. It was genuine remorse. He actually seemed sorry.

"Follow me," Sherman said as he turned from the doorway. He now was on a mission. We followed him out into the basement area. "We're gettin' out of here," he said. "And we're takin' these birds with us."

"How are we gonna do that?" Henry said. "Look at all of them."

"My uncle's got a truck," Sherman said. "He'll help us."

But before we could put our plan into action, we were rudely interrupted.

CHAPTER 14

The Knight School Caper

Sherman, what are you doing?" Olsen shouted. At least six-five, no, six-six, he was as wide as he was tall. He was even uglier without the wig and lipstick. He wore a short-sleeved white undershirt and dirty overalls. And he didn't seem happy to see us. I wondered how much he had heard.

Sherman stared at Olsen as if he were looking right through him. "You lied to me. You told me you were going to take these birds back to the wild and let 'em go."

"What do you care?" Olsen said. "You got paid."

"This is all wrong. I don't want any part of it anymore."

"Sherman, what happened to you? Yesterday you were just a big, dumb kid. Now you gotta get smart?"

"My friends and I are leaving. And we're takin' these birds with us," he announced.

"I don't think so," Olsen replied.

"I'm not gonna let you kill any more of 'em," he said.

As soon as Sherman uttered those words, I knew we were in trouble. All he had to do was play dumb. He had managed to do that every day of his life. Why not today?

"What are you talking about? I didn't kill any of them. Look in all these cages. They're as happy as can be."

"I'm not talking about *them*. I'm talking about the ones in the back room. The stuffed ones."

That was it—we were toast now. I admired Sherman for standing up to the old man, but couldn't he just have said nothing and let us go get help *after* we got away?

Olsen moved a couple of steps in our direction. We began to backpedal. He could see into the back room now, and by the look on his face, it was clear that he knew exactly what we had stumbled onto.

"You nosy brats!" he screamed. "Now you've done it. Now I can't let you go. You had to snoop around. Well, now it's gonna cost you."

"We won't say anything. We promise," Scarlett said.

"Oh, I know that. You won't be telling anybody anything. You're gonna stay down here till you rot."

"What are you gonna do with us?" Scarlett asked. Her voice was breaking.

Olsen placed his finger to his lips. "I know. I'm gonna add you to my permanent collection. All of you." He chuckled and began climbing the stairs, then stopped and turned toward Sherman. "If you're smart, you'll change your mind and join me. I could use a partner. You'll be the richest kid in town." He pointed to the three of us. "But you gotta help me do something with them first."

"No. No way. I'm staying here with my friends. I'm not helping you anymore."

"Suit yourself. I'll be back later tonight. I got a delivery to make. Maybe you'll come to your senses by then," he said as he climbed out.

We heard the cellar doors slam, and the chain slid back into place.

Scarlett promptly marched up to me. "This is all your fault. You got us in this mess. You better think of some way of getting us out."

"I was trying to reunite you with Socrates. And we did that."

"Well, you should have thought this thing through a little better." She began to cry.

I hated to admit it but she was right. I *had* underestimated this old guy. I should have listened to Eugene. He knew Olsen was crazy. He knew he was capable of anything.

Sherman approached Scarlett. "Don't cry. I didn't mean to steal your bird. I thought I was doing a good thing."

"Let's not worry about that now. We've gotta plan our escape," I told the others.

"How are we supposed to get out of here?" Sherman said.

"I doubt if we can bust out," I said. "But those doors are gonna open again—when he comes back to deliver some of these birds—that's when we put our plan into action."

"What plan?" Scarlett asked.

"That's the part I haven't figured out yet," I said.

She rolled her eyes.

"One thing I do know—when he comes back, we have to be ready for him. We gotta look around this place—cover every inch of it. Search for anything we might be able to use as a weapon. There's four of us and only one of him."

"Don't forget the birds," Sherman said. "Socrates and the other birds could help. They could attack him or something."

That was just the way we needed to be thinking. We quickly spread out and began our hunt. We had to find something. We just had to. I glanced at the others and felt a hollowness in my chest. I just couldn't let anything happen to these people. Scarlett had lashed out at me more than once but she had every right to. I should have listened to her grandpa and Eugene and stayed away from here. But, no, I'd wanted a taste of the big score.

I sat down, away from the others, and tried to concentrate. I wondered what Sam Solomon would have done in this situation. He usually found himself trapped somewhere in each episode—and he always managed to wriggle free. Yeah, like in Episode #13—*The Knight School Caper*—Sam was hired to find a fencing instructor who had disappeared. When Sam found himself too close to the truth, he was captured and left for dead in a walk-in restaurant freezer. Had he given up, he would surely have frozen to death. But not Sam Solomon. He immediately located the freezer's main compressor and disconnected it. Once the freezer shut down, it triggered an alarm that warned the restaurant owner that the freezer had failed. When workmen arrived to service the unit, Sam was able to escape.

I needed to come up with something just like that. Think, Charlie, think. But the more I did, the more I realized it was foolish. Sam Solomon was fiction. This was real. Sam always escaped. He had to. How else would the series have continued? This time it was up to me. And unless I came up with something, and fast, this might be our final chapter.

We decided to split up and conduct a thorough search of the area. After nearly half an hour, all we had managed to come up with was a dirty pair of sneakers, a broken lightbulb, some oily rags, a plunger, an old Mason jar, a sack of birdseed, some rope, and a garden hose.

"What good is any of this stuff?" Scarlett said. "We can't break out of here with this junk."

Scarlett was right. This was junk. I stared at each item hoping for some inspiration. I tried to imagine how we might combine one thing with another and create a weapon of some kind. But nothing was clicking.

"Well, I guess we could at least hook up that hose and blast Olsen with it when he comes back," I said. I looked around for a water source. I pointed to a sink on the far wall. "There's a faucet right over there."

"You're going to spray him with water? Now, that'd really hurt him," Scarlett said sarcastically.

"Well, I think it's worth a shot," I said. It felt good to have a plan. It seemed to give some of the others hope, but was it enough? A jet of water might startle him enough to buy us a few seconds, but we needed something else—we needed some sort of chaos. Some organized confusion. I thought hard for several seconds. Nothing was popping into my head. These people were counting on me. Come on, brain, kick in . . . please! And then something hit me. I thought about what Sherman had said earlier. "Don't forget the birds. Maybe they could help." Maybe they could at that.

"I just got another idea," I said. "When Olsen comes down to pick up the stuffed birds, we let him have it with the water. Then, get this, we open up all the cages and release the birds. Talk about chaos—it'll be mass confusion down here. And it might just give us enough time to slip out."

I was waiting for Scarlett to dismiss this idea as well, but instead she seemed to be staring off into space.

"Hold on, I've got an even better idea," she said.

"Oh, I can hardly wait to hear it," Henry said.

She picked up the bag of birdseed from the floor. "After we hit him with water, and after we release the birds, we toss this at him." She dug into the bag and pulled out a handful of seed.

"Birdseed?" Henry chuckled. "Now, that'll deliver a lethal blow for sure."

Scarlett glared at Henry. "Do you mind if I finish?" She sighed and composed herself. "Since Olsen will be soaking wet, the birdseed will stick right to him. And what do you suppose our little flying friends will do?"

I tried to picture the scenario that Scarlett had described. It was a great idea. No, make that a brilliant idea. "It's perfect," I said. "The birds'll head right for him."

"Dinner is served," Sherman said with a wide grin. It was the first time I had ever known him to make a joke.

"And that should give us just enough time to get away," I said. "Scarlett, I gotta hand it to you. You're starting to think like a real P.I." I turned to Henry. "What do you think?"

"I guess we can try it," Henry said. "What have we got to lose?" Under the circumstances, it was about as much of a compliment as Henry was willing to pay—considering it was Scarlett's idea.

"Hey," Sherman said. "You guys gotta let me man the hose. It's my fault we're all here. I want some payback."

"Then it's a plan," I said. "Henry and Scarlett, why don't you unhook the doors on the birdcages now, but don't open 'em yet. I'll wait by the cellar door. When I hear Olsen, I'll give you a cue. That's when you fling open those cage doors and release the troops. After that, it's your turn, Sherman. Turn that nozzle and let him have it. Then Henry and Scarlett can run up and cover him in birdseed." I needed to appear confident. If something bad was going to happen, at least we were about to give it our best shot. "We can do this, guys. You'll see."

The others appeared confident, but each of us knew the danger ahead. I shuffled over to the cellar door and waited. The more time passed, the quieter it got. None of us was in the mood for chatter. I could sense that with every minute we waited for Olsen to return, the more nervous we got. I decided to engage in conversation just to ease the tension.

"Hey, Sherman," I said. "Tell me something. When you were breaking into places to steal these birds, how come it never *looked like* you were breaking in? 'Cause— let me tell you—I personally checked both doors at the barber shop. There were no signs of tampering. It was almost as if you had a key."

Sherman smiled. He reached into his pocket and pulled out a handful of tiny tools. "I used these," he said.

I scooted over to take a look. I had never seen a set of tools like these before. There were at least a half dozen of them. Each one was about six inches long with a black rubberized handle. On the other end of each tool, there was a thin metal shaft with a bent tip small enough to slide into a lock. A couple of them had metal tips that actually resembled keys.

"The old man showed me how to pick a lock with these things. They worked like a charm."

And then I remembered something that Eugene had said in the barber shop the other day. It was all starting to make sense. One of Olsen's previous occupations was a locksmith. It was the perfect cover. With locksmith tools, you could enter a business clean as a whistle, make your heist, and walk away undetected.

"You won't be using them anymore, right?" I said.

"Heck, no." Sherman said. And he seemed sincere. "I don't ever plan on—"

Sherman stopped in mid-sentence. There had been a sound at the door above.

"It's showtime," I said. "Places, everyone."

Henry and Scarlett sprinted to the cages, threw open the doors, and began releasing the birds. Sherman ran over to the sink and turned on the faucet. I had to credit him with a brilliant suggestion. He decided that the water jet would be even more effective if we used the coldest water possible. Not only would it surprise Olsen, it would stun him as well. And Sherman was right. He repositioned himself on the floor in the middle of the cellar so as not to be seen right away. He fingered the nozzle on the hose. He seemed to be looking forward to this little altercation. Scarlett huddled in a far corner. I ran over and turned off the overhead light. It was dark. No, it was black. I held out my hand about six inches in front of my face. I couldn't see a thing.

I soon heard the chains being pulled from under the door handles. Moments later the cellar doors opened. Before anyone appeared, a familiar voice was calling out to us.

"How's everybody doin' down there?" Olsen said.

When I heard a thud, I knew he had entered the cellar. I aimed my flashlight right at him.

"Hey, what's goin' on?" the old man said. "Get that thing outta my face."

Olsen moved in my direction.

"Now!" I yelled.

A jet of ice-cold water shot through the air and nailed Olsen in the middle of the chest. He let out a pained yelp and fell to the ground. Sherman was relentless in his assault. A second later, Henry and Scarlett ran up and covered him with handfuls of birdseed.

"What do you think you're doing?!" he screamed.

The birds were now flying in all directions but

hadn't yet discovered the bonanza covering the old man. C'mon, you guys, we're counting on you. This had to work. It just had to. When Socrates finally landed on Olsen's head and began pecking at the seeds in his hair, it seemed to send a signal to his compatriots, who soon joined the feast. Within seconds, our captor was covered by his feathered friends.

"Go!" Sherman yelled. "Now!" He had turned off the water to avoid injuring any of the birds.

I grabbed Scarlett by the hand and led her past Olsen and up the stairway. Henry was right behind us. When we reached the cellar door, I pushed it open and looked out. The sky, filled with a million stars, was breathtaking. And the scent of the night air had never smelled better.

Scarlett was next to me, and Henry . . . but no Sherman. Oh no.

"Wait right here," I told Scarlett. "I'll be right back."

"What are you doing? We're free. Don't go back down there."

"I gotta get Sherman," I said. "Don't worry."

I snuck back down and flashed my light inside. Sherman was just about to make a dash for the door, but he had stopped for some reason.

"C'mon, Sherman," I yelled.

"I'm not leaving without Socrates," he said. "I owe him that."

Olsen was now sitting up. He was frantically waving at the birds, trying to shoo them away. But the little creatures were intense. No one, and I mean no one, was going to deny them a free meal.

Sherman hovered over Olsen, waiting for a chance to scoop up Socrates. He was trying his best to keep his distance from the old man. Sherman was a big, strong kid, but even he had no intention of tussling with a character as large and dangerous as Olsen.

"Maybe we should go get some help and then come back for the birds," I suggested.

"I'm not leaving without him," Sherman said. And I knew I'd never change his mind.

A moment later Olsen tried to stand but slipped on the wet floor and fell onto his back. That was when Sherman made his move. He crouched down and grabbed Socrates with both hands. Unaware that he had been snatched up by his rescuer, Socrates proceeded to peck Sherman relentlessly. But there was no way this determined kid was going to let go.

"I got him!" Sherman said.

"Okay, let's get outta here," I said.

I headed straight for the stairs, but as Sherman attempted to sidestep Olsen, the old man reached out and tripped him. He grabbed onto Sherman's ankle and held tight. Sherman started to kick and twist but Olsen's grip was firm. I held out my hand and Sherman took hold. I pulled and yanked and tugged, but I was no match for the stranglehold Olsen had on Sherman's leg.

"You're not going anywhere," Olsen said. "And neither are any of your little friends."

"Here," Sherman said as he handed Socrates to me. "Just go. I can handle him."

"No. We're all in this together."

Sherman tried to free himself but Olsen had him in what seemed like a death grip.

"Oh no!" Scarlett screamed. She and Henry had come back down to see what was delaying us. "Charlie, do something."

I handed Socrates to Scarlett and grabbed Sherman's right hand. Henry took hold of his left. We pulled as hard as we could but it was no use.

"This is never gonna work," Henry said. He let go of Sherman's hand, ran over, and picked up the hose. He pointed it at Olsen. "Let go of him right now."

Olsen chuckled. "Yeah, right."

"Let him have it," Scarlett yelled.

Henry moved the nozzle from side to side. He couldn't seem to get an open shot. "I'm afraid I'm gonna hit one of the birds." Then, as if they understood our predicament, two of the birds, apparently full, took flight—leaving a perfect target for Henry. He gripped the nozzle, pointed it at Olsen, and nailed him right in the face, causing him to lose his grip on Sherman.

Henry dropped his weapon and joined the rest of us as we sprinted up the stairs and into the back yard.

I breathed in the night air. This whole experience had been so crazy—no one would have believed it. But we had done it. We had actually done it. We were out. We were free. We were safe. At least I thought we were.

CHAPTER 15

The Grizzly Barefoot Caper

It was time to make a beeline for the highway and get as far away from this farm as possible. Everyone was present and accounted for—including Socrates. I noticed Olsen's blue pickup in the driveway. There was also a larger truck parked next to it. It was gray and looked like a delivery truck of some kind. I hadn't realized it at the moment but on our way out, Scarlett had apparently grabbed a small cage. She was busy stuffing Socrates into it.

"Okay, we gotta find the spot where we left our bikes," I said. "I think it's this way. C'mon."

"Wait a minute," Sherman said. "We're just leaving?"

Henry rolled his eyes. "Yeah, we thought it might be a good idea considering there's a psycho back there."

"But what about all those other birds?" Sherman said. "We can't just leave 'em here."

"We can't go back there now," Scarlett said.

But I knew Sherman was right. It was our duty—our responsibility—our mission—to rescue *all* the birds.

"It's too dangerous to go back," I said. "Our best bet is to go get some help. Then we can come back with reinforcements and save these birds."

"You're probably right." Sherman said, frowning. "I just hope they're still okay when we get back."

"That's a chance we'll have to take," Henry said.

"The sooner we get outta here, the better for all of us . . . including the birds," I said. "C'mon, gang." We paused for a moment to collect our bearings and then sprinted toward the front gate. With her arms wrapped around the cage, Scarlett was falling behind.

Sherman fell back a few yards to keep an eye on her. "Why don't you let me carry him for a while?" he said. A day earlier, none of us would have entrusted anything to Sherman, let alone our prized possessions. But this was a different kid now. Scarlett smiled and handed the cage over. She was now able to keep up with the rest of us.

We hadn't traveled more than a quarter mile when Scarlett pointed back at the house. "Look, he's coming," she whispered.

Olsen was in a full gallop, heading right for us. We had about a seventy-five-yard lead on him. If we could maintain that distance, we'd be okay. I ran until my ribs ached, never looking back. Every so often, we could hear the sound of high grass and bushes being trampled. My flashlight was long gone. I must have dropped it some-where along the way. We were fortunate to have a full moon lighting our path.

In the distance we could see the fence. At one point I didn't think my feet would carry me any further, but the sound of a pursuer is a great motivator. When we reached the gate, we began to search for the opening that Henry had cut in the fence.

"Where is it?" I said.

"Over here, I think," Henry said.

We could see Olsen bearing down on us. I scampered up and down the fence, frantically looking for our escape hatch. My heart was racing. The old man was within earshot now.

"Stay right there and you won't get hurt," he yelled.

"Maybe we should try to climb over it," I said. But I knew I'd never make it.

"Charlie, over here," Scarlett cried. She had found the hole and slithered through effortlessly.

Henry, Sherman, and I quickly followed. We continued running, desperately trying to locate the spot where we had left our bikes.

"I think they're by that big tree over there," Scarlett said.

What was she talking about? I couldn't see any tree. At this point, however, I wasn't about to argue. I let her lead the way. And lead us she did—right to the bikes.

We jumped onto our trusty steeds, then realized that Sherman was without transportation.

I slapped the rear fender of my bike. "Hop on, Sherman. We'll have to ride double."

"No," he said. "I'll just slow you down."

We could hear Olsen's heavy footsteps. He was breathing down our necks.

"I think we better split up," Sherman said. "He can't chase all of us. You three go ahead. I'll try to circle around and catch up to you later. Where are you headed? The police?"

"No," I said.

"Remember where you got Socrates from?"

"You mean the barber shop?"

"Yeah, there's an office on the second floor of that building." I looked back and noticed Olsen trying to crawl through the hole in the fence. He seemed to be caught. "We gotta go." I took the cage from Sherman and we were off . . . in opposite directions. I balanced the cage on the handlebars and wrapped my arm around it. It wasn't the most comfortable way to travel but there was no other option. I hoped it wouldn't slow me down too much. We concentrated on putting some distance between ourselves and our pursuer. We knew that since we had split up with Sherman, Olsen would now have to choose which of us to follow.

When we had traveled about five hundred yards, we

noticed Olsen on our trail again. He was slowing down however. After a few more steps, he stopped, turned around, and headed back in the direction of the house.

"Yes!" I screamed. "We did it."

"How can you celebrate at a time like this?" Scarlett said, pedaling furiously.

"Lighten up, would you?" Henry said.

"What's the problem, Scarlett?" I said. "We're all safe and Olsen's not chasing us anymore. That's great news."

"Have you forgotten about the birds, and what's probably going to happen to them when he gets back to that farmhouse?"

For a moment, I actually had. I felt horrible. I wanted to turn back and try to rescue them, but I knew that the best thing was for us to get to Eugene's and call for help. I wanted to defend myself but I decided not to, probably because I was too winded to speak. We rode as if we were trying to overtake the lead rider in a cycling race. I pedaled from a standing position the entire time, which wasn't easy considering I was still clutching the bird-cage. We managed to cover the terrain in what seemed like seconds.

"The barber shop's only about a block from here," Scarlett said.

We rode down a dark alley until we reached the shop. We ditched our bikes behind the building and entered through the back door. We flew up the stairs and Scarlett immediately knocked on the door.

"What are you doing? Eugene won't be here this late. And even if he was, he wouldn't answer," I said. "That's not the password."

"What are you talking about?" she said.

"Show her, Charlie," Henry said. "Show her how it's done."

"Another time," I said, "when we're not running for our lives. But right now, there's an easier way." I reached into my pocket and produced a key. I smiled confidently, slid the key into the lock, turned it, and pushed the door open.

"After you, my dear," I said.

"Nice," Henry said.

We entered the office, locked the door behind us, and flipped on the desk lamp. I set the cage with Socrates on top of the desk. Scarlett picked up the telephone receiver and handed it to me.

"Here, call Eugene," she said.

I just stared at it. Eugene still had one of those old-time phones that had to be dialed.

"Um . . . I don't know his number," I said.

"Call your grandma then," Henry said. "She'll know it."

"If I call my house, my mom or dad will answer. Then I'm gonna have to explain this whole thing. I'm not quite prepared to do that."

"They're going to find out eventually," Scarlett said.

"I know, but I'd rather tell them about it after we've wrapped up a successful case. That'll make it a little easier."

Scarlett put her hands on her hips. "Well, do *something*."

The sound of a door opening at the bottom of the stairs startled us.

"Who could that be?" Scarlett said. "Eugene maybe?"

"Or Olsen," Henry whispered. "Maybe he *did* follow us."

Scarlett let out a whimper.

I pointed to the desk. "Come on, we'll hide under there."

We crawled under the desk, huddled together, and held our breaths. Scarlett's eyes were closed tightly. We had locked the door. Olsen would have to break it down if he wanted to find us. How were we ever going to get out of this? How was it possible to overpower this brute? We had done it once. But there were no gadgets here to help us out a second time. It seemed hopeless. The building was empty. What if the worst actually happened? This wasn't the way I had intended to meet my maker. I had so wanted to reach my thirteenth birthday—the whole teenage thing and all. It seemed like it wasn't to be.

Tomorrow morning, Eugene would enter his office and make a gruesome discovery. It would easily be a front page story. The kids might even get a day off school. It would be a triple funeral. Now that would be a real spectacle. There'd be a line of cars a mile long. My mother would be in a black dress and veil. She'd . . .

Wait a minute. My mother. Of course. That was it. She was in my room the other day. And I remembered quizzing her about it. Now, if Eugene had truly laid out this office in official Sam Solomon décor, then I knew exactly what I had to do. I began banging on the bottom of the desk.

"What are you doing?" Scarlett said.

"There's a secret compartment under this desk. And if I'm right, there's a little something we can use to buy ourselves some time."

"What are you talking about?" she said.

There was no time to deal with hysterical civilians. I continued pounding. It had to be in here. It just had to.

"Maybe there's a button or a lever or something," Henry said.

There were no magic buttons. I knew that. All Sam ever did was apply pressure in a particular spot. Then right on cue, a flap would open and a can of sneezing powder would fall out. I can still remember reading in Episode #16—*The Grizzly Barefoot Caper*—when Sam tossed a handful of powder into the face of Joey "Papa Bear" Jacobson. The notorious underworld figure had surprised Sam in his office late one night. "Papa Bear" went into an uncontrollable sneezing fit allowing Sam to sneak out undetected.

We could hear someone climbing the stairs. All I

had to do was find this magic potion. Then if Olsen did break in, I'd have a little surprise for our uninvited guest. But first I had to find it. How could Eugene call himself an official Sam Solomon fan and not have a secret compartment under his desk? It was a disgrace. Everything else in the room was a perfect reproduction. How could he have missed such a crucial detail? It just had to be here.

"Think, Charlie," Scarlett said. "If it can help us, you gotta remember. C'mon, use your head."

Now that was an idea. Since nothing else had worked, I decided to do just that. I crouched down under the desk and banged the back of my head on the bottom of the drawer. And just like that, as if I had hit the jackpot on a slot machine, a tiny door opened, and its contents poured out onto the floor.

I kept waiting for a can to drop down, but all that fell out were dozens and dozens of . . . candy bars. There was every kind imaginable—ones with milk chocolate and dark chocolate and peanuts and almonds and caramel and marshmallows and . . .

"What's going on?" Scarlett said.

There was no sneezing powder. There was nothing here that would help us defend ourselves against this madman. I picked up one of the candy bars and threw it down onto the pile with the others.

"So much for watching your triglycerides, *Eugene*."

"Shhh," Scarlett said. "I heard something."

She was right. There was a voice outside the door.

I was expecting our pursuer to kick in the door but instead I heard what sounded like a key in the lock. But how would Olsen have a key? Wait a minute. Maybe he was picking the lock—with those tools Sherman showed us. A second later, the door swung open. I heard a voice. No, there were two voices. They were faint at first.

"Well, I get to pick the next movie. This one was a dog," a man's voice said.

"All right, all right, you made your point. It looked good in the commercial. What can I tell you," a woman said.

As the three of us remained huddled under the desk, I could immediately tell that the man's voice wasn't Olsen's. In fact, it was a very familiar voice. As was the woman's.

I popped up from under the desk and sheepishly said, "Hi, guys."

Grandma and Eugene seemed surprised to see us, to say the least.

"Charlie, what are you doing here?" Gram said. She pointed to the cage on the desk. "And where did this bird come from?"

A moment later, Scarlett emerged. Then Henry.

"What's going on here?" Eugene asked.

"Well, we've gotten ourselves into a bit of a jam," I said, "and we need a little help."

Before Eugene could respond, he spotted his stash of candy bars on the floor under the desk. "What happened?"

"I was looking for something . . . but I couldn't find it. All I found," I said, pointing at the candy bars, "were these."

"What were you looking for?" he said.

"It doesn't matter."

It didn't take Gram long to notice the candy. She folded her arms and stared at Eugene. "Why do I waste my time trying to help you keep your cholesterol numbers down?"

"Constance, I'm only human."

Grandma shook her head. It appeared she wasn't done lecturing Eugene. But before she could continue, we heard the downstairs door open again.

"There's someone out there," Eugene said.

"Uh-oh," I said, "he found us."

Eugene looked right at me with narrowing eyes. He didn't seem happy. "I'm guessing you know who that is."

"Well . . . kind of . . . listen, we better get out of here."

"Charlie, what's going on?" Eugene said. "Who's out there?"

"All right, I should have told you. We went over to the Olsen farm looking for Socrates."

Eugene threw his hands up. "What did I tell you about that?"

"I know, I know . . . but we hit the jackpot. We found

Socrates. See," I said, pointing to the cage. "And we also found all of the other stolen birds—some alive, some dead, some *stuffed*. Eugene, he's a black market taxidermist." I was almost afraid to continue. "You see, he found us in his basement and locked us in there. We escaped but now he's come back to shut us up."

We could hear heavy footsteps climbing the stairs.

"How will we get out of here?" Scarlett said.

"There's another exit," Eugene said.

"Where?" I asked.

"You should know. Any Sam Solomon fan should know. Does the Hudson Gang ring a bell? In fact, Sam used this escape in more than one novel."

The intruder was nearing the top step.

"Hudson Gang? What are you talking—" And then all at once it hit me. I ran over to the window and threw it open. I pulled the fake plant out of the flower box. And there it was—the rope ladder. I dug in for it and tossed it over the side of the building.

"Okay, gang," I announced, "let's do it."

"Ladies first," Eugene said.

Grandma smiled. "It's just like old times." She scooted to the window, climbed over the ledge, and began to shimmy down the rope.

Eugene motioned for Scarlett to go next.

She approached the window and froze. "Someone else go."

"Sweetie, don't be nervous," Eugene said. "You can do this."

Scarlett was not about to budge.

"Okay," the veteran P.I. said. "In that case, Charlie, go ahead."

"Henry, you go. I'll wait and help Scarlett."

Henry scooted to the window and effortlessly began his descent.

We heard footsteps approaching the door.

"Eugene, you better go next," I said.

Eugene reluctantly moved toward the window, tugged on the rope to make certain it was secure, and soon disappeared.

"I'll help you, c'mon," I said to Scarlett.

"I don't think I can do this."

"Of course you can. I'll be right here with you."

"Charlie, you don't understand. I'm afraid of heights."

"Just don't look down."

"Oh yeah, right. It's not that easy."

The doorknob began to rattle. I wasn't quite sure what to do. I knew that the chivalrous thing would be to wait until she was safely down, but that wasn't about to happen in the near future. And with Olsen only seconds away from gaining entry, I decided it best to get myself to the ground and then to gently try to coax Scarlett down.

I climbed out onto the ledge, and began to lower myself down the rope. I was worried about a rope burn, but even more concerned about losing my grip, and splattering onto the sidewalk. I could do this. I knew it. I had to make it. I had to. About five feet from the ground, I let go. *THUD!* I landed on my butt. I climbed to my feet and noticed Scarlett still in the window.

"Come on," I said.

She looked down and began to tremble. "I just can't do it."

The decision was quickly made for her when the intruder began banging on the door.

"Ahh!" Scarlett screamed.

"C'mon, honey, now!" Grandma yelled.

Scarlett stepped over the ledge and onto the top rung. She began to lower herself ever so slowly.

"You're doing great. Keep going," I said.

Halfway down, she froze. "I can't move."

"Don't look down," I screamed.

"Just leave me here and get some help. I'll be okay."

"I'm not leaving you. It's only a few more steps," I yelled.

"I told you I can't!"

"Look!" Eugene said.

There was a figure now standing in the window watching us.

"Hurry!" Grandma screamed.

Scarlett was about three-quarters of the way down when she suddenly froze. She clung to the rope with her eyes tightly closed.

"Jump!" Henry yelled.

Then, unfortunately, for the first time in her life, Scarlett actually listened to Henry. She just let go. I circled under her with my arms extended, hoping for the best. And then—*PLUNK!* She had landed directly in my arms. That was the good news. The bad news? My legs gave way and we both toppled to the ground.

She jumped up and brushed herself off. She could have at least said "Thank you." But instead, in the most sarcastic tone, she uttered, "My hero." I should have been offended, but under the circumstances, this was no time to feel sorry for myself.

"Hey, you guys left Socrates up here," the figure in the window called out.

It wasn't Olsen's voice.

"Sherman?" I said.

"You're not just gonna leave him here, are you?" Sherman said.

"You know that guy?" Eugene said.

"Well, yeah," I said. "He's the kid who's been stealing all the birds in the neighborhood."

"What?" Eugene said. He shot a confused look in Grandma's direction.

"But he's not doing that anymore," I said.

"Yeah, he's seen the error of his ways," Henry added.

"He's with us now," I said.

"He's okay. He helped us escape," Scarlett said.

Eugene shook his head. "So, now what?"

"So now we have to go back to the farm and save those birds before Olsen kills them."

"It's our duty," Henry said.

Sherman was now climbing down the ladder with one arm securely around the cage. Socrates wasn't making it easy though. He was squawking loudly and trying his best to peck at Sherman's fingers through the cage bars.

Grandma rubbed her hands together. "Time to get to work," she said with a smile. "C'mon, gang."

We followed her to the old Chrysler Newport and piled in. The cavalry was on its way.

CHAPTER 16

The Wok in the Park Caper

What do you think, Eugene? To the police station?" Grandma asked as she pulled out of the parking lot.

"There's no time," Eugene said. "We better go straight to the farm. If Olsen's been killing these birds like the kids say, there's no telling what he'll do now. He may be destroying the evidence as we speak."

"He better not be," Sherman said.

"Constance, do you know where we're headed?" Eugene asked.

"I know exactly where that place is," she assured him. "A lot of folks know where Olsen lives—if for no other reason than just to avoid him."

I was positioned in the backseat between Sherman and Henry. Scarlett sat in the front between Gram and Eugene. When the car pulled out onto the main road, we were suddenly thrown back as Grandma put pedal to metal. Eugene opened the glove compartment, pulled out a handful of maps, and threw them onto the floor. He reached in and slid out some contraption—it looked like some sort of radio—with lights and buttons and a small screen. There was also a handheld microphone attached to its side. It was the kind of mike you'd see on those old police shows. Eugene began playing with the dials and held down a button on the microphone.

"What's that?" I asked.

Eugene held up one finger. I needed to wait. He was now engaged in an important communication. "Captain Shamus to Chicken Bone. Captain Shamus to Chicken Bone. Come in, Chicken Bone. Over."

There was a short pause and then a voice responded, an older man's voice. "This is Chicken Bone. Nice to hear from you, Cap'n. What can we do for you? Over," he said.

"I need a favor. We have a situation requiring backup. We need to apprehend a suspect and deliver him to the nearest Smokey Bear. We're headed to the Rupert Olsen farm on Route Thirty-four. Over."

"Olsen?" the voice said. "What's that troublemaker up to now? Over."

"My sources indicate a black market operation of some kind," Eugene said. "Over."

"Wouldn't put it past him. Hey, Cap'n, what's your ten-twenty? Over."

"We just turned onto Old State Road Forty-seven. Over."

"What's your E-T-A? Over."

"About ten minutes, I hope. Over."

Grandma tugged on Eugene's sleeve and nodded in the direction of the radio.

"Oh, I'm supposed to say 'hi' from Mother Hubbard. Over."

"Well, a big howdy back to Mother Hubbard. And tell her I'm on my way. Wouldn't wanna miss this one. Over."

"I owe you one, Chicken Bone. Ten-Roger."

"So what is that thing, Eugene?" I asked.

"This, Charlie, is a CB radio. With everybody hooked on cell phones these days, not too many folks use these anymore. But there's still a bunch of us who just can't break the habit." Eugene smiled, set down the microphone, and slid the radio back into the glove box.

Flying down an abandoned rural highway proved to be the best ride of my life. The fastest roller coaster I had ever been on paled in comparison. Gram had no doubt participated in high-speed chases in the past. It was just like the ride that Sam Solomon experienced in Episode #19—*The Wok in the Park Caper.* Sam had discovered that a Chinese restaurant was actually a front for a ring of international jewel thieves. When Sam got a little too close, he found himself dodging pedestrians, bikers, and runners in New York's Central Park while bound and gagged in a runaway rickshaw. Like Sam and Gram, I welcomed the opportunity.

While we drove, we did our best to explain everything we had seen and heard while captive on the farm. Eugene no longer seemed upset with our decision to go out there on our own. He asked for specific descriptions of the farmhouse, the cellar, the surrounding fields, and Sherman's deal with Olsen. We told him everything. Soon the metal fence along the perimeter of the Olsen farm came into view.

"This is it," I said to the others. "Hold on to your seats."

Scarlett looked into the backseat and returned a nervous smile.

The Chrysler screeched to a stop at the locked gate.

"Now what?" Eugene said. "We'll never get through that."

I leaned forward. "We cut a hole in the fence about a hundred yards down. We can get through there."

"What do you think?" Eugene said to Gram.

Gram just smiled.

I had seen that smile before. I knew something was up. I made sure my seat belt was secure. I motioned for the others to do the same.

"What's up?" Henry said.

"You'll see."

Gram turned to Eugene and winked. "Just sit back, partner, and enjoy the ride." She put the Chrysler in reverse and backed up about fifty yards. She then seemed to point the vehicle directly at the front gate.

"You're not serious, Constance?" Eugene said.

Gram turned to face us. "Fasten your seat belts, kids."

And with that, she floored the accelerator. It didn't take more than a couple of seconds for impact to occur. We crashed through the gate effortlessly. Metal and dirt flew in all directions. A piece of the fence attached itself to the front bumper until it lost its grip a few yards later. The vehicle had sustained little damage except for a few scratches on the hood and a broken headlight.

"Where to, Charlie?" Grandma yelled out.

I pointed in the direction of the farmhouse. If the ride *to* the farm had been a rush, it was nothing compared to our trek over the open fields. Grandma, intentionally or not, managed to hit every rock, bump, hole, you name it. More than once, we hit our heads on the car ceiling, but no one seemed to mind. It was worth it to help stop Olsen from harming our little friends. Every so often Scarlett would let out a squeak. I couldn't help but wonder if she regretted joining us tonight.

It didn't take long before we reached the farmhouse. I immediately noticed that there were no lights on. Olsen must have killed the power after we got away. If I hadn't known exactly where I was headed, I'm not sure we ever would have found this place. The single headlight on the car provided our only means of light. We all piled out.

"Now where?" Gram asked.

I ran over to the basement entrance. The others followed. The doors leading to the basement were still open. Then we heard a sound coming from the truck parked next to Olsen's pickup. We ran over and found it filled with cages of squawking birds. Even some of the stuffed birds had been loaded in as well.

"He's getting rid of the evidence," Henry said.

"But at least the birds are still okay," Scarlett said.

"I'd feel a lot better if you kids got back in the car," Eugene said. "This character is still around here somewhere."

"I wanna help capture him," Sherman said. "This is all my fault."

"Son, I appreciate the offer, but I can't risk having any of you youngun's get hurt. C'mon, now, get back in there."

But before we could follow Eugene's orders, a figure emerged from the shadows.

"Is this a party or something?" It was our host.

Scarlett slid behind me. I could hear her breathing.

"Listen, Olsen," Eugene said. "I'm afraid it's over. We're taking you in. It'd be best if you just surrendered now. We've got reinforcements on the way."

Olsen laughed. "Yeah, right." He glanced in the

direction of the front gate. "You're bluffing. I don't see anybody."

"Trust me, they're coming," Eugene replied.

"I'll take my chances," Olsen said. "So it's me against all of you. To be quite honest, I like the odds."

"Don't be stupid," Gram said. "You're already in enough trouble."

"So what difference does it make then? What more can they do to me?"

Eugene glanced in our direction. "What did I tell you kids? Everybody in the car. Let me deal with this myself."

None of us moved.

"Get in the car," Gram said. "I'll stay out here with Eugene."

"No, I'm fine," Eugene said. "Trust me."

Scarlett made a beeline for the car. Henry followed. Sherman and I stood our ground.

"I can take him," Sherman said loud enough for all to hear.

"That won't be necessary," Eugene answered.

"You'll get your chance, Sherman," Olsen said, "as soon as I finish off the old-timers."

From the distance we could see headlights. Soon we heard the sound of a motor. Seconds later, an old station wagon, which actually looked more like a hearse, pulled up and screeched to a halt. The front door opened and out stepped a man who looked even older than Eugene or Gram.

"Good to see you, Chicken Bone," Eugene said.

"*He's* your reinforcements," Olsen said, laughing.

"Listen, Olsen," Chicken Bone said, "I've faced tougher characters than you. You don't scare me."

Olsen shook his head and chuckled. Then suddenly his expression turned serious. "It's too bad these kids have to see what's about to happen. You could avoid all that, you know. All ya gotta do is turn around and forget everything you saw here," Olsen said. "Or else, it ain't gonna be pretty."

Eugene now sported a determined look. He appeared ready to defend us with all the might that his scrawny body could muster. Eugene turned around and motioned for the rest us to get into the car.

It was at that moment, while his opponent was distracted, that Olsen made his move. He rushed Eugene and knocked him off his feet. I was halfway in the car when I stopped. Something suddenly came over me. For some reason, I wasn't nervous at all, and I didn't care what happened to me. I stepped out, slammed the door shut, and sprinted in the direction of Olsen.

But a few seconds before we were about to collide, Eugene, now on his knees, reached into his pocket and emerged with a handful of what looked like white powder. As Olsen came at him a second time, he tossed a handful of the powder into Olsen's face. The assailant stopped in mid-stride, then began to rub his eyes. He started to cough and choke. And then he sneezed . . . and sneezed . . . and sneezed. He couldn't stop. Chicken Bone ran at Olsen, knocking him over. Olsen fell onto his back. Chicken Bone rolled him over and pulled his arms behind his back. Gram then ran up and slapped a pair of handcuffs on him.

I smiled. So that was where the sneezing powder had gone. I knew that a real Sam Solomon fan would never leave the office unprepared. I ran over and helped Eugene to his feet.

"Sherman, we could use your help now," Eugene said. And so, Eugene, Sherman, and Chicken Bone dragged Olsen, still sneezing uncontrollably, and deposited him in the back of the station wagon.

"Chicken Bone, you follow us out of here," Eugene said. "On the way to the police station, we'll call Animal Control and ask them to get over here and take care of these birds."

Chicken Bone nodded and hopped into his car. Sherman decided to ride in the station wagon with Chicken Bone to offer a little extra muscle if needed. The rest of us piled into Grandma's car. As we drove to police headquarters, I couldn't believe that it was finally over. We had successfully rescued Socrates, as well as all the other birds. And we had helped break up a black market taxidermy operation. Not bad for a bunch of twelve-year-olds—and three pretty awesome senior citizens. I guessed that the birds that were still alive would soon be returned to their rightful owners. But there were some that didn't make it. It wouldn't be pleasant having to share the news of their demise.

Scarlett had joined Henry and me in the backseat. She held the cage containing Socrates on her lap.

I leaned over to her. "Case closed," I said.

"So, you really did it, Charlie," she said.

"But not alone." I smiled at Henry, and nodded to Gram and Eugene. "And don't forget Sherman and Chicken Bone."

Scarlett leaned over and kissed me on the cheek. "Well, now that Socrates is safe, how much do I owe you?" she asked.

I was feeling generous. "That smile is all I need . . ."

"Whoa, whoa, whoa," Henry chimed in. "That's my area if you don't mind. I'll take it from here." He turned to Scarlett. "So, Miss Alexander, here's how I figure it."

Scarlett rolled her eyes.

"I don't know what Eugene's cut is," Henry continued, "but if you consider research, legwork, surveillance, and expenses, and if you take inflation into account, the going rate these days . . ."

CHAPTER 17

The Dog Daze Caper

When we returned to school following spring break, it was hard to get back into the routine. Our lives had been turned upside down just a few days earlier. And there was a buzz throughout the entire school about the whole Rupert Olsen incident. The local newspaper had run a series of articles regarding the matter. The stories referred to a quartet of twelve-year-old heroes. We had become mini-celebrities. I think Scarlett enjoyed the attention the most. The only oddity was that the stories never mentioned the names of Eugene or Grandma. Though the articles did mention that a lot of the credit should go to two individuals whose identities would remain hidden, they were careful not to divulge their names. Chicken Bone, whose real name I never did learn, maintained his anonymity as well.

The police, as you might guess, were eager to question Olsen. In exchange for a lighter sentence, the accused not only divulged all of the gory details of his illegal bird business, he also provided authorities with a list of private collectors who had purchased his stuffed masterpieces. He even explained how he had duped Sherman into believing that he was performing a noble act by helping free all the caged birds. When the police were convinced that Sherman knew nothing about Olsen's illegal taxidermy business, and that he had actually helped the rest of us escape from our captor, they decided not to charge him at all.

As Henry and I waited at the bus stop after school that day, fellow classmates peppered us with questions about our ordeal. I thought it best to downplay our efforts. Henry, on the other hand, soaked up the glory. I was fine with that. When our admiring fans had finally disappeared, it gave us time to reflect.

"So what's next?" Henry said. "You gonna stay with Eugene permanently now?"

"Well . . . ," I said.

Henry appeared nervous. It was almost as if he were afraid to hear my answer.

"It only makes sense that he'd want you back," Henry said.

"I suppose now's as good a time as any to tell you," I said. I knew that would get his attention.

"Tell me what?" he said anxiously.

I looked around to make sure we were still alone. I knew it would help build the suspense.

"Eugene and I had a nice little chat on the phone last night," I said.

"And?"

"And he asked me to continue on at his agency," I announced.

Henry looked away, shuffled his feet, and avoided eye contact. He was clearly disappointed.

"I knew it," he said.

I don't think he was quite ready for the next words out of my mouth. "But I said that I wasn't interested."

Henry smiled. "What?"

"I told Eugene that I really appreciated the offer, but that after our little adventure, I now realized that the big score isn't all that it's cracked up to be. It's dangerous. A guy could get killed out there." I knew exactly what was going through Henry's mind at that very moment. He was picturing us back as a team, back in our garage, and back in business.

"You don't have to tell me the big score is no picnic," Henry said. "So, how did Eugene take it?"

"He sounded a little disappointed, but he seemed to understand. He told me that if I ever reconsider, he would welcome me back."

Henry leaned over to see if the bus was coming. "Well, I have to say—that was pretty nice of him."

"And he also asked if I'd think about joining him on a case-by-case basis. You know, if he ever gets in over his head and needs a little assistance."

Henry slid the backpack off his shoulder and dropped it onto the sidewalk. "So what'd you tell him?"

"I said *sure*. If you think about it, that's the perfect situation. Every so often, I get tired of these lightweight cases of ours. It'll be nice to have a chance to jump back on board for a real challenge—but just not every day."

And it was the ideal solution. The script couldn't have worked out better if I had written it myself.

"That *is* perfect," Henry said. "Sooooo, where does that leave us?"

"Back in business, if you want," I said.

Henry threw his arms into the air. "What are you talking about? Of course," he said excitedly. "You know, I'm really glad to hear you say that—'cause I booked a client for today."

I shook my head. Had I heard him correctly? After a near-fatal experience, we had a little R & R coming. No need to jump back into the saddle so quickly.

"You did what?" I said.

"I know that your mom always does her grocery shopping on Monday afternoons. I figured it was okay."

The unmistakable rattle of Grandma's clunker put an end to our conversation. She pulled up to the curb and rolled the window down. "Get in, gents," she said.

"I didn't know you were picking us up today, Gram. Mom didn't say anything about it."

"She's not privy to classified information. Hop in."

"Henry too?"

She nodded.

I have learned over the years never to argue with Gram, even if I have no idea what's happening. Henry and I jumped in the backseat. Gram proceeded to the entrance of the school playground and stopped.

"Anything wrong?" I asked.

"Nope. Just gotta pick up another fare."

"Who?"

"You'll see."

And just like that, we noticed Scarlett running to the car. She got in the front seat next to Grandma.

"What are *you* doing here?" Henry asked.

Scarlett shrugged. She apparently had no idea either.

Had we somehow become embroiled in yet another mystery? The three of us said nothing. We waited for Gram to enlighten us, which never happened. We drove through town wondering what could possibly be up. We eventually pulled into our driveway and waited for the answer.

"Everybody out," Gram said.

We stood on the sidewalk in silence, awaiting our next order.

"I'd like to have a little chat with the three of you—in there," she said, pointing to the garage.

We entered through the side door and waited for Gram to spill the beans.

"I might as well just spit it out, boys. Charlie . . . Henry . . . I would like to nominate Scarlett here for induction into your private detective agency."

We looked at each other in dismay.

"Gram, I didn't know Scarlett was interested in joining us."

"Why don't you ask her?" she said.

I turned to Scarlett. "Well . . . are you?"

Scarlett seemed confused. "I've never actually considered it."

"See, she doesn't want to join," Henry said.

Grandma placed her arm around Scarlett's shoulders. "I saw you in action the last few days, dear. You're a bright young lady with great intuition. Charlie and Henry could use someone like you. You should think about it."

"Well," Scarlett began, "as scary as it all was, I have to say that I did kind of enjoy myself. I guess I wouldn't mind helping out here . . . if they want me, that is."

"You don't sound too convincing," Henry said. "And you'd have to prove yourself."

"I'm just going to leave you kids here to discuss things," Gram said. "You know how I feel. Give it some thought." She smiled and slipped out.

An uncomfortable silence followed. The thought of seeing Scarlett not only in school, but working at the agency each day, was dizzying. I wasn't sure if I could concentrate with her seated right next to me. But I was willing to give it a shot. To be honest, I wasn't certain if Scarlett possessed the necessary skills to be a real private investigator, but I certainly wasn't going to veto her joining us. Henry, on the other hand, would undoubtedly put up a fuss. Convincing *him* that she was qualified would be the toughest challenge.

"So, now what?" Scarlett said. "Do I have to take a test or something?"

Henry thought to himself for a moment. "Yeah, that's a good idea."

"We don't have any tests to give her," I said.

"I just thought of one," Henry said. "Here goes— a cowboy rides into Dodge City on Sunday. He stays three days and raises a ruckus. The marshal asks him to leave. So he rides out of town on Sunday. How is that possible?" Henry sat down in a lawn chair, crossed his arms, and smirked.

Scarlett seemed puzzled. "He rides in on Sunday, stays three days, then rides out on Sunday?"

"Yeah, that's about it," he said.

She thought hard for a couple of minutes. Henry's smile got wider as each second passed.

"I don't know." Scarlett placed her hands on her hips. "And that's just what you were hoping for, isn't it?"

"I'm just trying to see if you measure up, that's all."

"Well, the whole thing is stupid," she said. "Who cares about some dumb riddle?"

"It's not some dumb riddle," Henry said. "It's a test

of your deductive reasoning skills. And they gotta be operating at peak performance to work here."

"So, what's the right answer?" she said.

"Charlie, would you like to do the honors? If you know the answer, that is."

"I haven't heard this one before . . . but . . . if he rode into town on Sunday . . . stayed three days . . . and rode out of town on Sunday, there's only one possible answer."

"And that is?" Henry said.

"Wait a minute," Scarlett said. "I got it."

"Be my guest," I said.

"His *horse* was named Sunday," she announced.

Henry groaned.

"Well, looks like she passed," I said.

Henry was having a hard time processing what had just happened. "Yeah, she passed the *first* test."

"Aw, c'mon," I said.

Henry was now deep in thought. He was determined to come up with another riddle—one that was guaranteed to stump Scarlett. But a knock on the door suddenly put this oral exam on hold.

"It's not over," Henry said as he pulled out the card table and opened it up.

I quickly set up a couple of lawn chairs. "Scarlett, please let our next client in. And, by the way, welcome to the team."

"She's not in yet," Henry said.

When Scarlett opened the door, I was shocked, to say the least. Standing there was Sherman. And, you know, I was actually happy to see him. That wasn't always the case. Had he shown up on our doorstep a week or so ago, I would have shuddered.

"I got an appointment," he said.

"Come right in and have a seat," I replied.

Sherman dropped into the lawn chair across from the desk.

"So, what brings you here today?" I asked.

"We got a little problem at home, and I thought you might be able to help."

"I'll do my best," I said.

Henry and Scarlett pulled up chairs and sat on either side of me.

"We just bought a new house," Sherman said.

"That's good, right?" Henry said.

"Yeah, but I'm having a problem getting our pets to the new house."

"What sort of problem?" Scarlett asked. She was fitting right in.

"Well, we have a dog, a cat, and a mouse."

"That's an interesting combination," Henry said.

"Here's the problem. My dad doesn't allow any of the pets to ride in the car, so *I* have to move them to the new house. On my bike. And I can only carry one at a time."

"So what's the big deal?" Henry said. "Make three trips."

Sherman frowned.

"Is there any reason you can't do that?" I said.

"Well, yeah. We can't leave the dog alone with the cat 'cause they'll fight if no one's around. And we can't leave the cat alone with the mouse . . . or no more Mr. Mouse, if you know what I mean."

Scarlett grabbed a legal pad from the card table. She started jotting down some notes.

"What do you think?" I asked her.

"Why don't you ask me?" Henry said.

"I will . . . in a minute."

"I'm not sure," Scarlett said. "Every combination I come up with won't work."

"Okay, Henry, how would you solve this?"

"How the heck should I know? I just wanted you to ask me first."

"I'll ask you first next time, okay?"

Henry nodded.

Apparently it was up to me. I tried my best to visualize the process of transporting the animals in such a way as to avoid bloodshed. Every time I thought I had reached a solution, I realized that it was faulty. Then I thought about Sherman's problem in a different way—not just moving the pets from the old house to the new one, but actually moving one or more of them back to the old house if necessary, and then returning them to the new house. A minute later, I had it.

"Okay, Sherman, try this: First, you need to take the cat to the new house, and leave the dog and the mouse at the old house. Then go back to the old house and take the mouse to the new house."

"That won't work," he said. "They can't be alone together."

"Let me finish. You take the mouse to the new house. And you take the cat *back* to the old house. Then you take the dog to the new house, and leave him with the mouse. Finally, you can go back to the old house and pick up the cat and take him to the new house. You might get a little tired of all the trips, but the pets will arrive happy and healthy. What do you think?"

"My head is spinning," Henry said.

Sherman seemed to reflect on the proposed solution for a minute. "You know, I think that just might work." He reached out to shake my hand. "How much do I owe you, Collier?"

Right on cue, Henry ran over to the workbench and returned with the money jar.

I waved him off. "Sherman, after everything we've been through the past few days, this one's on the house."

Henry threw his head back and groaned. It was a familiar sound.

Sherman lifted himself out of his chair. He was

smiling. "I appreciate that. Okay, then, I guess I'll see you guys at school tomorrow."

He was barely out the door when Henry began shaking the jar in front of my face.

"How are we ever gonna make some money if you keep giving away the store? And have you forgotten?" he said, nodding in Scarlett's direction. "We may have *three* mouths to feed soon."

"Oh, so does that mean you've given your blessing for Scarlett to join the agency?"

"Not quite," Henry said. "She's gotta pass another test."

Henry wasn't making this easy. In the event that Scarlett failed his next quiz, I somehow had to convince him that the inability to solve a brainteaser shouldn't prevent someone's admission to the Charlie Collier— Snoop for Hire agency. But how could I make that happen? I thought about it for a minute, and then it hit me. Who better to set the example than Sam Solomon?

Sam was certainly no stranger to partnering up with a new associate whenever he found himself in a jam. He did it a bunch of times—like in Episode #9—*The Dog Daze Caper*. In this particular case, Sam was hired by a woman who wanted him to find out why her French poodle had suddenly become aggressive. Sam knew he was no animal behaviorist—so he teamed up with one. And with her help, he soon discovered that a local veterinarian, whose business was failing, was behind it all. The vet had apparently drugged a number of expensive purebred dogs during routine office visits. Later, when the owners called to report the animals' sudden aggressive behavior, the vet convinced them that their dogs had contracted a rare virus which had caused them to go mad. He offered to euthanize the animals at no charge. When the unsuspecting owners dropped off their pets, the vet injected them with an antidote which cured them. He then sold the high-priced canines for a tidy sum. If Sam hadn't teamed up with a new partner, he never would have figured it out.

I was now armed with the ammunition I needed. If Scarlett was to fail Henry's next test, I was prepared to share this particular Sam Solomon tale. I was certain I could make him see the light.

"So, are you all ready for your final exam?" Henry said.

Scarlett sneered at Henry and shot me a disapproving glance.

"Listen," I said to Scarlett, "if it were up to me, you'd already be in. This isn't my idea."

Henry gritted his teeth, and was just about to fire away when a knock at the door diverted our attention.

I looked at Henry. "Did you book anyone besides Sherman?"

"No," he said.

"Then who could this be?" I said.

"I don't know."

"Why doesn't someone just get that?" Scarlett said. When neither Henry nor I responded, she shook her head, sighed, and opened the door.

I think it's safe to say that none of us expected to see the person who was standing in the doorway.

"Eugene?" I said. "What are you doing here?"

"Your grandma told me I'd find you kids in here."

"What can we do for you?" I said.

"Listen, Charlie, I know you told me that you prefer working here and solving cases for your friends, and I can respect that. But you also said that you wouldn't mind helping me out on occasion. Is that still the case?"

"Well, yeah," I said. "Whenever you need some extra muscle, you can count on us."

"I'm glad to hear you say that," Eugene said, "because I need you."

"Really?" I said.

"Just Charlie?" Henry said.

"No, I want to hire all of you. I need three more sets of eyes and ears for a pending case."

"Wow," I said. "What's it all about?"

Eugene closed the door and spoke softly. "Yesterday I got a call from . . ." He paused. "Let's just say . . . from someone who shall remain nameless."

We looked at one another and smiled nervously.

"It seems there's a problem at . . ." Eugene paused again. "At a location that shall remain nameless."

"This sounds really important," I said. "So, what exactly is the problem?"

"The problem is regarding a subject . . . that shall remain nameless. So, are you kids with me?"

"To be perfectly honest," Henry said, "I'm a little confused."

Eugene smiled. "How about if I explain everything to you tomorrow? At my office. After school. How's that sound?"

I had no idea what we were about to agree to, but I knew that Eugene would never put us in harm's way. I tried to imagine what Sam Solomon might have done under these circumstances. I knew that he'd never let a friend down no matter how mysterious a case appeared to be.

"Count me in, Eugene," I said.

"Me, too," Henry said.

It was now Scarlett's turn to chime in. We'd soon find out just how committed she was to all this cloak-and-dagger stuff.

"If you really think I can be of some help, I'd love to," she said.

"Scarlett, Charlie's grandma and I both think that you'd make a great addition to this team. What do you say?"

"In that case," she replied, "I'm in."

"Great," Eugene said. "So, I'll see all of you tomorrow at . . . shall we say four o'clock?"

We looked at one another and nodded our approval.

Eugene turned to leave, then hesitated. "I shouldn't even have to say this . . . but not a word to anyone. This is a matter of national security."

"Don't worry," I said.

Eugene winked, threw open the door, and disappeared.

And just like that, we found ourselves about to embark on a new journey—one that promised to be more exciting, more suspenseful, and undoubtedly more dangerous than the last. We had no idea what to expect. Eugene had been tight-lipped. And perhaps that was best. One never knows who may be listening in on a private conversation. I was fairly certain that our garage had not been bugged, but who really knew for sure? In his line of work, One would assume that Eugene performed frequent and painstaking sweeps of his office in search of listening devices. It made perfect sense.

I wondered what sort of adventure was awaiting us. All Eugene had said was that it was a matter of national security. I could only guess that it involved double agents, diabolical plots, and international intrigue. Would I be up to the challenge? Were the others aware of exactly what they were about to undertake? Either way, we had accepted Eugene's invitation—there was no turning back now.

So, yours truly, Charlie Collier—Snoop for Hire, my partner, Henry Cunningham, and our newest team member, Scarlett Alexander, are about to be tested . . . again. Will we ultimately prevail? Only time will tell. Will we turn back the forces of evil? We can only hope so. Will we get on each other's nerves? Umm . . . I'd rather not say. And who knows, if the business continues to grow, we may be looking to add another associate to the agency someday. Perhaps, someone like you. But in order to be considered, you'd have to pass a series of tests. Tell you what—consider this as your first exam. Here goes: Can a man in Illinois legally marry his widow's sister? Think about it. Real hard. Read it again—slowly. Can a man in Illinois legally marry his widow's sister? Do you have a guess? I hope you said that since she's a widow—then he's dead. The answer is no. Congratulations! You've passed the first test. You're almost a full-fledged member. But there are more tests to come. So keep solving brain busters. And keep sharpening your powers of deduction. 'Cause you're gonna need 'em.

Stay on the case with

CHARLIE COLLIER

as he investigates

The Camp Phoenix Caper

CHAPTER 1

The Cereal Killer Caper

Henry impatiently tapped on his watch. "She's late. I can't believe it. The first day of our new three-man agency, and she's late."

"Correction," I said. "Two-man, one-woman agency."

"Whatever."

"Relax," I said. "There's probably a perfectly good reason for it."

"Like what?" Henry refused to let it go. "Charlie, I told you this was a bad idea. We don't need her."

It was no secret that Henry and Scarlett would never be considered BFFs, but they both had something to contribute to this agency, and I had to do my best to keep the peace between them, for all our sakes.

"I thought you were over all of this," I said. "Let me remind you that Scarlett comes highly recommended."

"What are you talking about?"

"Both my grandma and Eugene suggested that we

take her on. Don't you remember? They were impressed by the way she handled herself in the birdnapping case. They thought she just might make a nice addition to our little detective firm."

To be perfectly honest, I could understand how Henry felt. He was probably worried about getting squeezed out. The Charlie Collier, Snoop for Hire partnership had been a two-man operation from day one—Henry Cunningham and yours truly. With the addition of a new associate, namely one Scarlett Alexander, I'm sure Henry felt that he might slip a notch in the chain of command.

"Well, she better get here soon," he said. "We don't have much time."

He was right about that. With my dad at work and my mom at the beauty salon with Grandma, there was no telling how long we'd have the garage to ourselves.

Henry picked up a handful of darts and began tossing. "Let me know when she gets here," he said disgustedly.

I for one was excited about Scarlett joining up with us. Not only would she add another brain to the mix, but the thought of being this close to her each day was dizzying. I only hoped I could concentrate. Oh, don't worry, I'm a realist. I know that a kid like me—one who closes his eyes when he steps on the scale—could never end up with a girl like Scarlett. But stranger things have happened. When she sees me in action each day—when she's able to witness my amazing powers of deduction—when she watches me solve cases with little to no effort—then who knows? Sparks could fly. But I'm not holding my breath. If I were only as suave and debonair as Sam Solomon, then things would be different. That's Sam Solomon, Private Eye, if you're wondering. It's a series of detective novels set in Chicago in the 1930s. I've read every one in print. I consider myself not only a fan of the master detective, but a student as well. I credit Sam with helping me sharpen my reasoning skills. I only wish he could help me sharpen my social skills.

"Ooh," Henry cried. "I missed the bull's-eye by a quarter inch."

Before I could congratulate him, there was a knock at the door.

"Finally," he said as he tossed the remaining darts at the board.

"Come in," I said.

When the door opened, I tried to maintain my composure. I didn't want to look too eager.

"Hi, guys," Scarlett said as she entered. "Sorry I'm late."

"Oh, that's al—" I started to say.

Henry was somewhat less forgiving. "That's it? *'Sorry I'm late'*?"

"Something came up. Is that all right?" she snapped. "Something important."

Henry sighed. "And if you just happened to be on a stakeout, and you just happened to show up late, and you just happened to miss the perp in action, are you gonna say 'sorry I'm late'? It's unacceptable. Tell her, Charlie." He folded his arms and smiled confidently.

Scarlett placed her hands on her hips and glanced in my direction.

I was well aware that once Scarlett joined the agency, I'd be breaking up squabbles between these two on a daily basis. I was prepared for that. But in this particular instance, I was being asked to take sides. The wrong move here could haunt me for a lifetime. I paused to think it over. On the one hand, Henry was right—punctuality in our business was important. But he also needed to understand that trust was equally important. Sometimes you had to give someone—in this case, a business partner—the benefit of the doubt. I had to handle this in a delicate manner.

"Henry, I'm sure that Scarlett would have been here on time if she could have," I said. "Right, Scarlett?"

"Of course," she said.

"And I'm sure that she had a very good reason for being late," I said. "Right, Scarlett?"

Scarlett began tapping her foot. She didn't look happy. "Why don't you just ask me why I was late? I know you're dying to."

"I don't want to pry."

"Well, I do," Henry said. "What was so important?"

I pulled a lawn chair out from under the card table and motioned for Scarlett to sit down. We needed to deal with this in a civilized manner.

She reluctantly lowered herself into the chair. We joined her at the table.

"Well?" Henry said.

"Would you believe we had a flat tire?" she said.

Henry's eyes narrowed. He seemed skeptical. "You can do better than that."

"It's true," she insisted.

I needed to seem supportive, even though it did seem like a pretty lame excuse.

"Flat tires happen, and there's nothing you can do about them," I said. "Let's move on."

"Not so fast," Henry said. "I want to hear the details."

Scarlett sighed. "Not that's it's any of your business, but all right, I'll tell you. We were driving on Thiry-Third Street when we heard this thumping sound, and the car started to pull to one side."

Henry folded his arms and made a face. He wasn't going to make this easy.

"So my mom got out and noticed that the front passenger's-side tire was flat," she continued. "We didn't want to have to wait around for the motor club, so we decided to try to change it ourselves. I'd watched my dad it do it before."

"You should become a novelist," Henry said. "This is some of the best fiction I've ever heard."

"For your information," Scarlett said, "I happen to know what I'm doing. I opened the trunk and took out the jack and the lug nut wrench."

The expression on Henry's face suddenly changed. He knew as well as I did that people just didn't throw out a term like *lug nut wrench* if they didn't know what they were talking about.

"So we popped off the hubcap, loosened the lug nuts just slightly, jacked up the car, took the lug nuts completely off, and set them in the hubcap."

Henry was speechless. She *did* know what she was talking about.

"We got the spare tire from the trunk, put it on . . ." She sighed. "And that's when the trouble started."

"What do you mean?" I said. "It sounded like you were doing everything right."

"Everything was perfect until my little brother decided that he wanted to help. So I told him he could hand me the lug nuts. He was so excited that he ran over, but he accidently kicked the hubcap, which sent the lug nuts flying. They ended up in a ditch somewhere on the side of the road. We were never able to find them. So then we had to wait for the motor club." She glanced at Henry. "Are you happy now?"

"Whatever," he said. "Let's just get to work."

I would have been perfectly fine with doing just that and putting this squabble behind us, but I kept thinking about that flat tire. I figured that there had to be a way to solve the problem even with the missing lug nuts. I thought about it for another minute, and then I had it.

"You didn't have to call the motor club," I said. "You had everything you needed to put that tire back on."

"What are you talking about?" Scarlett said.

"All you had to do was take one lug nut from each of the three good tires, and use those. Then you could have replaced them later."

"Yeah," Henry said. "And you could have been here on time. Just see that it doesn't happen again."

Scarlett slid her chair out and stood. "It's not going to be like this every day, right? Because if it is, I want no part of it."

I needed to do something, and fast. I was not about to let Scarlett walk out that door. Partner or not—best friend or not—Henry was being unreasonable and someone had to tell him. It was just like what happened to Sam Solomon in Episode #15—*The Cereal Killer Caper.*

In this particular story, Sam was investigating the owner of a local diner who was suspected of trying to poison one of his customers with a tainted bowl of cornflakes. Sam immediately sought out the services of two old friends, a husband and wife team of chemists, to analyze the fatal feast. They were good—very good—but they were always at each other's throats. The mismatched lovers, whose expertise Sam desperately needed, were constantly trying to sabotage each other's findings. In time, Sam was able to convince them to put their petty jealousies aside and to work together for the good of the client.

And suddenly I knew precisely what I had to do.

"Scarlett," I said, "please sit down. Henry, I have to be perfectly honest—I can't take this either. If we spend all our time arguing, we'll never accomplish a thing. We might occasionally disagree on what strategy to employ on a particular case, but if we're constantly bickering, then we're doing our clients a disservice. Scarlett is an official associate of this agency, and we have to work together—no matter what." I stood up. "Now, I want the two of you to shake hands. It's the only way."

Scarlett extended her hand. She was willing to bury the hatchet. Henry, however, just sat there with his arms folded.

"Henry, we can't move forward until we put this behind us," I said.

Without making eye contact with Scarlett, Henry sighed and reluctantly shook her hand. It was a weak effort on his part, but at least we had made some peace. Neither of the combatants, however, looked too pleased about it.

I knew this was about as good as it was going to get

for now, so I decided to take advantage of the cease-fire and move on.

I rubbed my hands together. "Okay, what's on the docket for today?" I asked.

Henry reached over his shoulder and grabbed a legal pad off the workbench behind him. He glanced at it and then held it up for both of us to see. The page was blank.

"No clients?" I said.

"Nada," Henry replied.

"Then what are we doing here?" Scarlett said.

"Not everybody makes appointments," Henry said. "We do take walk-ins, you know."

Scarlett got up, walked over to the door, and opened it. She stuck her head out.

"You're right," she said. "There's a long line of people out here."

Henry jumped up and ran over to see. There was no one.

Scarlett flashed a devious smile.

"Real funny," Henry said as he slammed the door shut.

Here we go again, I thought. I needed to maintain some order. "Listen, I thought we had a truce. C'mon, both of you, sit down. Let's get to work."

"What work?" Scarlett said. She picked up the legal pad off the card table and held it up.

"We have other business to discuss," I said.

"Whatever happened with that thing that Eugene was talking about? I thought there was something going on. The other day when he was here, he said something about a big case that he needed our help on. What's up with that?" she asked.

"Yeah," Henry said. "What about that?"

I knew what they were talking about, but I didn't think they'd like the answer. Shortly after we had wrapped up the Rupert Olsen birdnapping caper, Eugene had shown up and had asked us to join him on a new case—one he described as *a matter of national security*. We were all excited about helping out, but we never heard anything more about it. So a couple of days ago, I rode my bike over to Eugene's office to ask him about it. It was now apparently on the back burner.

"I spoke to Eugene about that case just the other day. It's on hold for the time being."

"Why?" Henry asked. "What happened?"

"Something else came up. Something bigger. Eugene got called away on a special assignment," I said. When Uncle Sam called, Eugene—despite the fact that he was in his eighties—dropped whatever he was doing to report in.

"What kind of assignment?" Scarlett said. "To where?"

"All he said was that he'd have to get back to us on this other case and that he needed to brush up on his Portuguese."

"He's headed to Puerto Rico?" Henry said.

"No, not Puerto Rico. Portugal, probably," I said.

"Or Brazil," Scarlett added.

Before I could compliment Scarlett on her knowledge of world languages, I heard a car engine in the distance.

"That's my mom," I yelled. "How could they be back this soon?"

Henry looked at his watch. "It's only four fifteen. I thought your grandma had a four o'clock appointment."

I quickly folded up the lawn chairs and hung them on hooks on the garage wall.

"She did," I said. "Something must have happened."

Henry broke down the card table and slid it behind a ladder. "A little help over here, if you don't mind," he said to Scarlett.

"Well, I've never done this before. I don't know how you guys do it," she said.

"Scarlett, you'd better take off," I said. "I'll see you at school tomorrow." I didn't have to tell her twice.

She shot out the side door and disappeared.

Henry and I followed. Before exiting, I grabbed a football from one of the shelves.

"What's that for?" Henry asked.

"We need a cover. C'mon, let's make it look like we've been here for hours."

The instant we slammed the door behind us, we could hear the garage door opener.

"We're lucky," I said to Henry as I tossed the football in his direction. "If my mom had seen Scarlett, she would have asked all kinds of questions."

Seconds later, Gram and my mom walked out of the garage and into the backyard.

"Hi, boys," my mom said.

"Hi, Mrs. Collier," Henry said.

"Back so soon?" I said.

"You won't believe why we're early," my mom said. "No more than a minute after your grandmother sat down in the chair, there was a robbery."